# the flower queen

A 1970's Suspense Romance Novel

The Flower Queen
Book One

## kay freeman

# acknowledgments

I want to thank Jason Pettus, my editor, for his invaluable contribution to making my books the best they can be.

I also extend my heartfelt gratitude to my Beta readers, Baylee Humphries, Susan Keller, and Meghan Marshall. Your dedicated time, effort, and insightful comments have been crucial in shaping my characters.

Lastly, thank you to my readers for continuing to purchase my books. Without your support, none of this would be possible.

Cover Credit: Bookcoverzone

# content warning

<u>**Age 18+ Conten**t</u>:

Both the hero and heroine are survivors of psychological and physical trauma. She's a victim of child abuse, due to neglect and was a victim of a house invasion and a rape. He was a victim of abuse from an over-bearing father and deals with dyslexia and witnessed domestic abuse. The heroine makes the difficult decision to grow marijuana to save her family farm after her husband dies from cancer. The book also contains graphic scenes of sexual acts. If you find any of this objectionable or triggering, stay clear. However, with all this said, the book is healing and hopeful and ends with a positive, loving relationship between her and her boyfriend an FBI agent.

# **contents**

# 1
# levels of hell

Marnie

"Which level of hell is this?" I ask. Nothin' in the mailbox but bills. If I hadn't been such a coward and skipped picking up yesterday, it wouldn't be like a waterfall today, with envelopes falling everywhere in cascades. I hold my breath and reach through the driver's-side window to collect them. The one on top is from the Josephine County Tax Office. Property taxes are always sent out April 30th. I rip the top open like I do when removing a plastic bandage from a cut—fast, in the hopes of minimizing the pain. I check the amount due and bite my lip. "People like me always fall short and hard," I grumble. Opening the bill fast made little difference. I still owe money I don't have. *Crap.*

I shove the paper into my jean jacket pocket, slam the box shut, and stamp the accelerator hard. In a few seconds I'm out of my driveway and streaking down the highway as strands of my hair whip around me. For a brief few seconds, and the first time in three years, I'm satisfyingly alive. When I drive fast, all those thoughts of what will happen if I don't pay go away. The sun is shining and the temperature is sixty-seven degrees, as I head toward the city of Grants Pass in Oregon, away from my farm and my troubles.

To most people, Grants Pass would seem like paradise. The town's slogan is, "It's the climate," printed on billboards throughout the area. Usually, opening a story with the weather is lame, but in this case my livelihood depends on growing things, and from now on it will become more so. I'll eventually become known as The Flower Queen. It has a nice ring, don't you think? I much prefer it to what people used to say about me—the poor girl whose mother was murdered. The word "poor" in my case does double duty. I started out with nothing…and I still have most of it. For me, sarcasm is not an attitude, it's an art form, and it's my secret weapon for surviving in this world.

I'm late for my part-time job as a waitress, which is normal. It's after 7:15 am as I park my old Chevrolet pickup in an open space in front of Ruby's Diner. I take one more hit off the reefer and listen to the tail end of a Donna Summer song before pinching it with my fingers and squeezing it out. Ruby's was the only game in town for breakfast and lunch in 1978 and it will be another four years before there's anywhere else to go.

I've worked at the diner part-time to supplement my family's income for over fifteen years. If you know anything about farming, you understand it's not always dependable because of various factors. In my case, my husband Jack factored into the unreliability. He's now become even more unreliable, because he's dead. It wasn't his choice and I can't blame that on him like I did many other things. People think dying is hard. It's actually helping people live that's difficult. It was three years from the time Jack was diagnosed with pancreatic cancer until he died. He tried all kinds of treatment, and I was his cheerleader. He wanted to give up after one year. I pushed him through year two. By year three, he was begging me to let him stop. I'll probably go to hell for not letting him.

The plate glass window at Ruby's is clean and sparkling. Carl, the owner, takes pride in the restaurant and comes in early or stays late to ensure the panes of glass on the windows and doors are clean of all fingerprints. He said once, "I don't eat at places with dirty windows." I've since adopted the same philosophy. If the owner doesn't care about the front of the place, what shape is the kitchen in? I step across the threshold and see that the rest of the establishment is in its usual tidy condition too. The black and white checkerboard floor smells slightly of oranges. The red vinyl booths, stainless steel chairs, and Formica tables are spotless and just beginning to fill. "You're late, Marnie," Carl yells. The scent of roasted coffee beans, pork products, and hashbrowns frying on the grill hit my nose next, mixing with the orange scent as I reach the row of stools.

"This is the time I always come in," I bark back at him. He can't argue with the truth and slinks back to the kitchen. I could be on time if I wanted to. I'm a very efficient person even though I smoke pot. I've had to be, with working here, being a mother of twin boys, and being the wife of a disorganized farmer who had a terminal illness.

I wrap my clean white apron around my waist and shove the pad and pencil in the front pocket. Sharon—Carl's wife—Kate the other waitress, and I start pouring coffee and handing out menus to patrons who've already claimed tables. It's first come, first served at Ruby's. Kate and I have been friends since kindergarten, and when our eyes connect, I don't have to say a word to her. She senses I've got something important to tell her because of the way I squeeze my eyes close and shake my head.

At eleven-thirty, once the breakfast crowd clears, we take our break and head out back by the green-colored dumpsters covered with graffiti. Even in our small town, the teenagers have something to say. "Charlie's Angels Rule" is written in bold graffiti on the side of one of the dumpsters. "Spill," Kate says after lighting her smoke and blowing several perfect smoke circles that disappear in a blue sky dotted with cotton candy clouds.

I pull the tax bill out of my jeans pocket. I would never tell anyone else, but I have to share with someone. "This came yesterday." I pass it to her. "I don't have the money. You know Jack didn't leave me a thing but his debts. No life insurance, nothing."

When Kate takes the paper and reads the amount, her eyes grow huge. "What are you going to do, Marnie?" She takes a drag off her smoke and doesn't wait for me to answer. "Maybe you should sell the farm, get out from under. Do you really want to slop around in pigshit until the day you die without any help?"

I scoff. "Don't sugarcoat things on my account." I turn my back on her.

Kate takes my shoulder and spins me around. "It's the truth, isn't it?"

"It's not about me. The land is a legacy. It's been in Jack's family for generations. It's for Chester and Cole. If I sell it, what will they do?"

"Ask them."

"I did. Chester wants to farm and Cole—"

"Let me guess," Kate smirks. "Cole wants to get the hell out of Dodge and become a hard rock musician or a tattoo artist, or maybe move to Jamaica and become a Rastafarian."

"Something like that," I snicker.

"I'm sure you'll come up with a plan, or I will." Kate throws her smoke on the ground and grinds it down with her hot pink patent leather platform shoe. How she works in them all day, I have yet to learn, but she triples my earnings in tips. It's more than just the shoes; her cheerful attitude and short skirts contribute to it too.

She grabs my hand and drags me back to the diner. We head through the kitchen and begin to enter the seating area until I see him and stop. I hardly recognized him at first...he's all grown up. He looks like a movie star. Sharon shows him to a booth by the order pickup area. I duck behind the warming station and hide, remaining in the kitchen. Kate doesn't; she pushes the double doors, enters the dining area and makes a beeline for him.

I can't face Wayne Farr after all this time. He's handsome, and I'm a mess. I avoid looking in mirrors as much as possible. After Jack got cancer, I didn't have time to take care of myself even if I'd wanted to. The inside of me is another story. I'm frozen at age fifteen forever, thanks to what happened to my mother and me.

"Coffee, please," Wayne says, his eyes glued to the breakfast side of the menu.

"What are you doing back here, Wayne? I thought you left forever." Kate giggles in that flirty way she has. Even I think it's freakin' adorable.

Wayne pulls his head up, surprised. "Kate, is that you? Oh my gosh, I apologize, I didn't recognize you."

"Do I look that bad?" Kate asks with her pencil shoved into the corner of her mouth. Like she ever could. What a joke.

"No, of course not." Wayne blushes and stands up. He was always a gentleman. "It's the opposite. I mistook you for a teenager." His dark brown hair is styled different; no longer in a pompadour, swept up high on the top of his head. It's now clipped short and tight on the sides. He's even more handsome…

"You're such a sweet-talker." Kate slaps Wayne's shoulder. "So what are you doing back in town? It's been years."

"I just got a transfer from Portland, to be closer to my dad. Since my brother passed some years ago, he's in need of companionship."

"Ahhh. You're a good son. I heard he was having trouble. What do you do?"

"A government job."

"Did you hear about Marnie?" *I'm going to kill you if you say another word, Kate.*

"What about her?" I peek over the counter. His eyes are wavering back and forth, concerned.

"Her husband died and she's all alone out on that big ol' farm." *I am not. I have Cole and Chester and a pack of dogs whose number grows daily.*

"When did this happen?" He gets an expression on his face where he might bolt, run out of the diner and drive there.

"A month or two ago."

"Someone told me she has twin sons," he says as he sips coffee.

"True. They're sixteen now."

"How is Marnie handling it?"

"Which part, the death or having teenagers?" *Jesus, Kate.*

Wayne laughs lightly and shakes his head. "Actually, I guess both. Are they well-behaved boys, I hope?"

"Both of them have genius IQs. The one boy, Chester, is a happy-go-lucky, dreamer type, like the father. But the other one, Cole, is like Marnie, analytical and a planner." Good dodge, Kate. She didn't tell Wayne how Cole's plans sometimes lead to trouble. He's already been arrested twice. He's something of a hothead, too, and takes offense quickly. "You remember how Marnie was so even-tempered after—"

"You mean emotionless and withdrawn." Wayne shakes his head and lowers it. "She had her reasons, of course. No one lives through what she did and not have it affect them." He stares at his coffee cup.

"So what would you like?" Kate changes the subject and has her pen poised to write.

"Poached eggs, I guess." He taps the closed menu.

"On toast?"

"Yes."

"Okie-dokie, Adam and Eve on a raft. Bacon or sausage?"

"Bacon and some hashbrowns, if you have them." *What diner doesn't have hashbrowns?*

"Watching your figure?" Kate laughs. "I'll put the order in." She walks away, hands the ticket to Carl, looks down and crosses her eyes, and sticks out her tongue at me.

"You better stop talking about me," I whisper. Kate ignores me and returns to Wayne with the coffee pot.

"More coffee?"

"Sure."

"I can't believe they never caught anyone," Kate says as she tops off Wayne's coffee and makes eye contact with him.

"I don't like to talk badly of others, but the police didn't do a professional job collecting the evidence. They corrupted the crime scene." How does Wayne know this? Did his father, a policeman, tell him? I regularly call the police, and the latest detective, a new one every year, never confesses they screwed up, but I've always had my suspicions. They always tell me they're working on it, but I know they're lying. They want me to be quiet and go away.

"She's never been the same. You know what I mean?" Kate says. That's the understatement of the year. She knows I'm listening, or she'd say more.

The bell rings. "Order's up," Carl calls to Kate, then turns to me and asks, "Aren't you working?"

"No, I have to wait."

"For what?" Carl asks with raised eyebrows as I crouch on the floor.

"For Wayne to leave."

Carl wrinkles his nose and tilts his head to one side. "He better be a fast eater."

Kate places the plate with Wayne's breakfast in front of him. He shoves a forkful of egg in his mouth, takes a bite of toast, chews and swallows, and then looks at Kate severely. "You've got to remember I lived through it; I dated her. Would you expect Marnie to act otherwise? Her mother was murdered and they've never found the perpetrators. If they had DNA, they might have a chance someday. They're making advances all the time. But without it, I don't think they'll ever solve this." Wayne retakes his cup and grimaces. "She never wanted to leave the house. I had to beg her to do so. And even then, if we went anywhere and she didn't like the looks of someone, we had to leave. I can only imagine what she..." Wayne stops talking and eats some more potatoes and Kate watches him.

I still don't go out much, and it's been over twenty-six years. Even here, when I wait on someone, I check them out. I check their age, height, the color of their eyes, and whether they have a scar.

"She takes a lot of security precautions. Her farm is a fortress. Marnie has more weapons than the militia." That's an exaggeration, but Wayne doesn't know that and makes a face like you see in a horror movie; his mouth and eyes open large, and his eyebrows shoot up.

I do have some weapons. I sleep with an S&W Model 19 under my pillow and an AR-15 under my bed. For backup, I have a machete by my nightstand, and when I leave my house there's a Buck knife in my boot. I reach down, checking to ensure I have it now. I have an ax in the truck under my seat and a smaller snub nose in the glove compartment. Kate didn't mention the bear spray deterrent I always keep in my pants pocket as well. It's not for bears, of course. They aren't the problem. It's people; men in particular.

"She's got dogs and motion lights." Kate nods her head. "She'll probably really step it up now that her husband's gone."

I hadn't thought about it as much as I should. My son Cole seems to be on top of it, though. He likes guns, too. Maybe a bit too much. I've already gotten several calls from school. They don't appreciate how he dresses in camouflage, or the long black coat, or the bleeding people he draws on the front of his notebooks. They want him to see a psychiatrist. I defended him. I told the school, "The drawings mean nothing. Don't judge him by his clothing. It's what's in his heart that matters." He would never hurt another family after seeing how my life had been altered by the murder of my mother.

Wayne finishes his food and pushes his plate away. "Do you think I should call her?" I can't believe he wants to call me after hearing all the talk about guns. Isn't he afraid of getting shot? What's wrong with the man?

"Why not? She liked you, Wayne, she really did. It's just, you know, everything that happened..." *Stay out of it, Kate. Don't encourage him.*

"They say timing is everything in life. Would you be comfortable giving me Marnie's number?" *Don't, Kate, please...*

"Sure." She writes on the bottom of his check and passes it to him. Damnit.

"Thank you. Wonderful seeing you, Kate." Wayne stands and hugs her, revealing that he's even more muscular than before. I'd pulled away when he had hugged me after it had happened. I didn't mean to, but he was so tall, and he reminded me of one of them.

"You too, Wayne. If she doesn't call you back, don't take offense. It might be too soon after her husband's death."

"Gotcha. You're a good friend, Kate." Wayne walks to the register, and pays. The bell rings as he leaves, and then he's on the sidewalk, passing the front of the diner window before disappearing. He's even more handsome than he was back in high school. He's a man now, his face more angular, his jaw square. He's got beautiful lips. *Stop it, Marnie.* He's taller than any of the other men I've ever dated. He was a super jock back then, on the varsity basketball and football teams. He went to college on a football scholarship. After he went away, I cut him loose. He was three years ahead of me and things wouldn't have worked. I didn't like feeling overwhelmed; I didn't need the pressure. I dated someone shorter and less intimidating after him. Then I met Jack, and he wasn't intimidating at all. He didn't seem to care about anything, not even me. I think that's why I married him; no pressure.

"Marnie, get out here. He's gone. What's wrong with you?" Kate asks, snapping me out of my thoughts.

"You know the answer to that question."

"Wayne wanted to see you."

"You shouldn't have given him my number."

"Well, I did. If you don't want to speak to him, don't call him back. I've also got an idea about your other situation; we'll talk about it in your truck when our shift is over at three o'clock."

Everything's good until two, when a customer comes in and freaks me out when ordering. I run to the bathroom and Kate soon follows. "His eyes are green," I explain, my words echoing in the tile bathroom.

"Calm down, Marnie. Plenty of men have green eyes."

I don't want to peek, but I can't stop myself. I look out and close the door quickly. "But he's also the right age. The man would be in his late forties now."

Kate's shoulders slump. "I can't believe you're doing this to yourself." Kate hoists herself onto one of the vanity sinks. "You can't keep going down this road over and over. You promised you wouldn't examine every man who dined here."

"I thought I could, but I can't, and he's got a scar on his hand and—"

She jumps off the counter. "You promised." Her forehead wrinkles. "I know the man. He's nice. He owns the airport. You're going to go out there, apologize, and serve that man his hot roast beef, mashed potatoes and gravy. That's all there is to it."

"But I can't. I've already made a fool of myself and—"

"It doesn't matter. If you don't, Carl could fire you. Do you want that?"

"I'll get another job."

"Not in Grants Pass, you won't. Everyone's heard about your issues, and there are no other waitressing jobs. Carl's been good to you. Now get out there."

Kate's right, of course, on every count. I sigh and open the restroom door.

"Order up," Carl yells. I head to the window. Carl's face is full of worry as I pick up the plate. The grief I've caused Carl over the years, and he's never given me so much as a warning or a tongue lashing. I approach the man I earlier accused of raping me and deliver his food. I hold my breath before setting it down. I notice Carl has given the man extras of everything. The plate is so heavy I have to lift it with both hands.

"I'm sorry about what I said. I thought you were someone else." The man's mouth twists, but he doesn't glance at or say anything to me. He picks up his fork and starts eating his meal. His eyes aren't really green, more a hazel color, and the scar on his hand is nowhere near his thumb. Why did I think he was the one? "More coffee?" I ask.

He nods and asks, "Can I have more creamers, too?" in a soft voice.

"Sure, I'll fetch some." The man finishes his meal, asks for his check and even leaves a tip without further incident from me.

The next hour passes quickly, which is one of the reasons I like working in the diner; I'm too busy to think about anything…most of the time. At three o'clock, Kate and I yell, "Bye, Carl," grab a soda and head for the door. I'm relieved I made it through another day without killing anyone.

KATE AND I WALK TO MY TRUCK. I SEARCH MAIN STREET. I'M ALWAYS on the lookout for trouble. There's not much here but the essentials: a laundromat, a small grocery store, Ruby's, a hardware store, a five-and-dime where teenagers hang, the bank, and a couple of attorney's offices. Off the main drag, we have a record store, a bookstore, a beauty salon, a police station, and a barbershop. Further outside of town are several bars, keeping those attorneys in business. Things don't stay open late like in the cities, except for those bars. It's small-town America; people want to go home to their families during the week.

My Chevrolet is faded brown, rusty, and beautiful in its ugliness. There are even holes in some of the rust, reminding me of Swiss cheese. It's the kind of truck you don't have to worry about. If someone hits me, so what? But others know by looking at it that I have nothing to lose, so they stay out of my way. I collapse against the torn seat, worm a finger in one of the tears, and pull some stuffing out to calm my nerves. "Stop it, Marnie," Kate says, slapping my hand. "One of these days, you won't have anything left to sit on."

"I'm nervous." I reach for the baggie under the seat and pull out the lighter and one of the joints I've rolled. "This will help. I'm going to try to cut back now that Jack's gone." The joint sparks. I take a huff and pass it to Kate. She takes one puff, coughs, and covers her mouth. "What does cutting back look like for you? Five times a day from ten?" And winks, "Do you think smoking so much contributes to your paranoia?"

"What paranoia? I'm perfectly calm."

"If that was you being calm back there with that customer, I don't want to see you wound up."

"Let's not talk about it."

Kate nods. "How much pot do you have left from the plants you grew for Jack when he was sick?"

"I don't know exactly. I'd have to weigh it, but I grew over fifty plants. I could have seventeen pounds or a bit less."

"If you got rid of it, it might help you cut back."

"True. I'd like to set a better example for the boys."

"They know you smoke it?" Kate's mouth falls open.

"I don't smoke in front of them. They might have smelled it. They're not stupid, but they're too polite to say anything."

Kate nods her head. "You always had a green thumb. Too bad your husband didn't listen to you more. If he did, the farm would've made a profit, instead of losing money left and right. Just a thought, but you should weigh it. According to Billy Sage, you can get between six hundred and eight hundred dollars per pound depending on the quality and whether it's buds, stalks or seeds. "

"Who's Billy Sage?" I ask.

"A friend of mine."

"You didn't give him my name, did you?"

"Of course not. I'm not stupid."

"It's illegal to sell marijuana, Kate."

"It's illegal to grow it, too. And stop playing with the window." She gives me another swat. "How many times are you going to roll it up and down? I'm surprised you haven't broken it already."

"It's just a nervous habit." It's like several other nervous habits I have that I can't stop doing, even though they don't make sense.

"You have a choice." Kate stares at me. "Sell the marijuana and pay your tax bill, or lose your farm. Pick one." She brings me close, squeezes me, climbs out of the truck, walks to her car, turns, and waves.

I sit there momentarily and swipe the blunt against the metal door until it's out before turning the key in the ignition. The engine stutters and doesn't engage. I try again. This time, the engine catches. I signal, put the truck into first gear, steer it from the curb and drive towards the orange sun.

The farm is all I have and will ever have. I think about the place I call home, and turn the idea of selling pot around in my head, as I watch the big orange ball in the sky sink lower and lower as my thoughts do, too.

I HEAR MY DOGS BARKING WHEN I PULL INTO THE DRIVE AND TURN OFF the engine. I walk down the small stone path that leads to the kennel my husband built. It took me three years to raise enough money for the materials. I held bake sales, and Carl and his wife donated a big chunk. My son painted the building red before Jack died. It provides inside kennels and outside runs. I have ten dogs right now, the most I've ever had. I don't go looking for them; they find me. People drop them off at my house, bring them to the diner, or tie them to the truck's bumper when I have it parked somewhere. I can't say no to them. There's a local shelter, and I have nothing against it. Still, they can only take so many, and unfortunately, they euthanize. I don't do that. I could never make those kinds of decisions between death or life for one dog or another.

The dogs, mostly pit bulls or pit bull mixes, stop barking as soon as I enter. They all run to the front of their kennels, jumping up and down and wait for me to stop in front of them. I pet each one and talk to them. I take Happy out and he jumps on me, almost knocking me down, licking my hands and face. He's all white with tan freckles. I snap a lead on and sneeze immediately. It's his turn to come in the house tonight. I notice the hives on the inside of my wrist by the time I reach the door.

# 2
# homecoming

<u>Wayne</u>

The house and yard don't look the same. My father was obsessed with ensuring our place was the nicest on the block. He insisted we mow the grass at least once a week. If my brother Mark or I missed a spot, he harangued us and made us do it again. It appears it's been a good long while since anyone's touched this grass; in some other spots there's nothing but dirt and weeds remaining, as if no one's watered it.

The house is another matter. The paint has faded boards. There are peeling spots on the windowsills, and the windowpanes are covered with dust and grime. There's an old car and an even older decrepit truck parked in the driveway, leaving no space to park, not even for me. The truck is up on cinderblocks, missing two of its tires. Where did these vehicles come from, and how long have they been here? Now this house is the shame of the neighborhood. I'm glad I accepted the job so that I'm around to check on things more.

I walk up the sidewalk and around the broken pieces of cement. Why did my father let the house fall into disrepair? He's got Social

Security and a pension from the police department. He can afford to have this stuff fixed even if he can't handle the repairs himself.

I seldom talk to my father anymore. He says I ask too many questions and don't act like I used to. I don't keep my mouth shut; that's what he means. I had to when I lived with him, because if I didn't, he punished me. After I left for college, I never went back, not even when my mother and then my brother died. I still remember the night I got a phone call from my father about my brother. "I've got bad news, Wayne."

"What news?"

"Your brother didn't make it."

"What are you saying?"

"Mark was in a car accident Friday night. Unfortunately, he was drinking and driving. He hit a tree two blocks from home. Fortunately, no one else was hurt. The services are on Friday."

"This is all your fault!" I yelled.

"You don't mean that," my father said.

"Yes, I do. If you hadn't laid your hands on him and Mom, he never would've started drinking in high school."

"I admit I made mistakes and—"

"If you weren't a cop and those cops weren't your buddies, you'd have gone to jail for touching him. I won't be attending. I'd have to pretend I love you, but I don't and never will. The only reason I'll ever come back is to arrest you and make you pay for what you did to Mom and him."

"But son, listen—"

"No, I'm not listening. Those days are gone." I ended the call.

But now I'm here, and I'm filled with regret for not being there for either of them, my mother or my brother. I was a terrible big brother. Why didn't I know my brother started drinking again? I should've died instead of him. I slip the key in the door, but it doesn't turn. My father must've changed the lock. I ring the doorbell instead, but that doesn't work because I don't hear it ring. I knock a few times, and then I bang harder, but no one answers.

The neighbor next door, my best friend's mother, pokes her head out the window, her face upturned, with eyes that sparkle. "Hi, Wayne," she says. "Wallace is around back. He probably can't hear you." Her voice is bubbly. All the kids on our block wanted to go to Gary's house because of his mom. You always felt welcome there. It wasn't just the pool, or that she made cookies, gave out the best Halloween candy, or told legitimately funny jokes. It was her. If you had a problem, Mrs. McGuire took the time to listen.

"Thank you, Mrs. McGuire. How's Gary?"

"He works for the police department now." My brother Mark wanted to go into law enforcement, too. She smiles. "Gary's married with three children, all girls."

"Wonderful. Tell him hello."

"Are you married yet yourself, Wayne?"

"Hmm, not yet."

"What are you up to? Trouble, I bet." She winks.

"A government job." I wave, smile, and walk around the side of the house. I spot him, the subject of all my childhood nightmares. He's hunched over, a shriveled old man. I wave. "Pops, I'm home."

He turns around and glares. "Wayne, where's your brother?"

"Let's go in the house and have a soda pop." Jesus. My father has lost it if he doesn't remember Mark's been dead for over twenty years. He's the one who told me Mark had been drunk and caused his own death. I didn't believe him and still don't. Mark joined AA the year before and hadn't touched a drop in a year. What had caused him to start drinking again?

My father leads the way to the back door, and we enter the house. The inside is even worse than the outside, something you might envision from someone with a hoarding problem: kitchen counters piled with newspapers, old tools, empty pizza boxes, gallon milk containers, and many other items that should've been thrown away a long time ago.

My father goes to the refrigerator, pulls out two cans of off-brand root beer, and hands me one. "Follow me," he says, and we head down the hallway. There are books, and boxes of tools piled there. The living room is messy, too. There's nowhere to sit until my father takes a chair and empties the contents onto the floor by tilting it. He does the same thing to another chair and lowers his compact form into the broken, stained damask rose club chair. My mother's chair. My father isn't the overwhelming, dangerous figure he once was, the one I feared bringing my failing papers home to that required a parent's signature. "You're a dummy; you need to try harder," he'd say. *I need to work harder and longer because I'm defective and not the same as everyone else.*

"Why are you here, Wayne?" my father asks, his eyes glazing with suspicion. I take in the bear head still hanging over the fireplace. I've always hated it. I remember my father hunting with his police buddies. He was so proud he'd killed a black bear. "A giant specimen," my father had boasted when he'd arrived home. I'd felt shame. How hard is it to kill something when you outnumber it and have a gun? Bears aren't aggressive by nature. They just want to be left alone to protect their young. They only defend themselves when backed into a corner. This one didn't have a chance with men like my father and a bunch of other half-drunk yahoos with high-powered rifles. When my father had the bear's head sent to the taxidermist, mounted and displayed over our fireplace, and I had to view it daily, it sickened me. When I complained, my father called me a sissy.

"Why are you here? Where's Mark?" my father asks again when he sees me still staring at the bear.

"I have a new job in Portland. I thought I'd drop in and check on you. Don't you remember that Mark is…dead? That he died years ago?"

"Liar!" my father stands and yells. "Come back when you want to tell me the truth."

"I want the truth too, about Mom. Tell me about Mom."

"I don't want to talk about her, the slut." My father's face has a sheen of sweat, and it's reddening.

"Dad, that's not true." The framed certificate on the wall reads "Lieutenant Wallace Farr." I remember how proud he was of becoming a lieutenant. He'd received the promotion two weeks before Marnie's mother was murdered.

"It's true!" he screamed, his hands jerking and one forming into a fist. "I'm not sure you're even mine. Now get out." I stare at my father, a man I'm supposed to honor. I exit the front door and sit in my car.

A black and white pulls in behind me and parks. The officer climbs out of his car, comes to my window, and leans in. "Wayne, it's been a long time. I can't believe you're here." Gary holds out his hand.

"Me too. Way too long. It's good to see you, Gary." We shake hands. The rain starts coming down in dribs and drabs. "Why don't you climb in and we can talk?"

"Sure, Wayne." Gary walks around to my Dodge and climbs in the passenger side. "My mom called and said you dropped by to see your dad. It's a good thing you did. He's been acting strange. A couple of neighbors are complaining."

"What's he done?" My gut tightens as the rain hits the windshield harder.

"He starts fights. Accuses people of taking his things. Tools and lawn equipment he hasn't owned in years."

"I'm sorry." I'm light-headed. It's worse than I thought. I should've come back sooner.

"Have you thought about putting him in a..." He lets his thought deliberately trail off.

"A home? Are you going to bring reinforcements to help?"

"You think he'll put up a fight?"

"Don't you? He still has a full gun rack in there, and a survivalist's compound full of ammo. He still doesn't like me much, either. I thought I could ask him some questions about my mother, but he isn't in any condition to answer them, or maybe he just doesn't want to. Maybe you can help me."

"Help talk him into leaving?"

"No, I don't think he'd listen to you or anyone else. I'm looking for a copy of my mother's file. You wouldn't be breaking any rules.

I'm pretty sure I could order it through the Freedom of Information Act, but my father's involved and it's a closed case. It might not look right to people here."

"You better believe it wouldn't." Gary won't look at me and stares out the window instead. "Your own father, Wayne?" He glances around the car. "He's a retired police officer. A confused old man now. Where's this going to lead?"

"I hope it'll lead to the truth. I can decide later whether to pursue it."

Gary puts his hands up. "If you had questions, why didn't you do something about it back then?"

"I was in college, and I feared him, and my brother was still living in the house. I couldn't take a chance. You're one of the few people who knows my father wasn't what he pretended to be; not Mr. Law and Order, on the side of justice. He was a monster. He would've retaliated. You know that."

He sighs. "I agree, but I just don't understand what you're going to do about it now, even if you do discover any wrongdoing. You're just going to stir everyone up and make everyone in the department resent you. Your father has a lot of friends, people who like and respect him."

"I have friends too. You, for example. I hope." The rain is falling harder now, and I turn on the wipers.

Gary looks toward the even darker clouds. "Alright, if you're hellbent on this, I'll filch a copy for you. But if anyone asks how you got it, you don't say it was me. Are we clear?"

"Absolutely. I promise."

"It's good to see you again, regardless. Have you seen Marnie?" Wayne lowers his voice to one of sympathy.

"No, but I plan on it." A clash of thunder sounds and a bolt of lightning flashes, lighting up the grey sky.

"Be careful." Gary's eyes water. "One of her sons is the protective type. With the husband just having passed, who knows how the kid is thinking."

"I'll be careful. When do you think I can have that file?"

"I have to take my time. There's a storage room for old cases next to the evidence room. I have to make sure both it and the copier room are empty at the same time."

"Perhaps I can ask for another favor."

"Shit, Wayne…"

"I realize I'm asking for a lot, but what can you tell me about Marnie's mother's case?"

"I wish there *was* something I could tell you. They have new detectives working it every year, but no one's gotten anywhere. I stop by Ruby's most mornings, and it kills me to have to face her." Then Gary changes the subject. "How about you, Wayne? Do you like your job?"

"I love it, but sometimes I don't think I'm good enough."

"What?" he says with a scoff.

"You know, because of my disability."

"You call dyslexia your disability. I call it your secret weapon. You notice things other people don't, and your memory is sharper than anyone else I've ever met."

"You think so?"

"Yes. Don't you?"

"I've never thought about it that way. I've just seen all the ways it's held me back over the years, especially what a curse it was in school."

"Some of the teachers in our high school weren't too helpful," Gary admits.

"That's the truth. You'd think being educators, they'd care, but some of them didn't give a shit. A few passed me just because they wanted to make sure I could play in the state finals. My father didn't help me either. He'd say, 'Nobody cares about losers, only winners.'"

"I knew you struggled and your dad was a jerk, but I didn't know it was that bad."

"Ah, forget about it. It just used to drive me crazy when things came so easily for the students who didn't even try. They never did a lick of homework, and I used to spend hours trying to read a paragraph."*It's what caused me to make the worse mistake of my life.*

"I had no idea."

"Those are the same people wasting their talents today because they don't want to work. They'd rather collect unemployment or pick up a welfare check."

"Come on, Wayne, do you really believe that?"

"Yes. Some people don't want to work. Things came easily to them when they were young, and they expect it to stay that way forever." It'll never get any easier for me. *I'll have to work hard to redeem myself for what I did if I ever can.*

"So where and what are you working on now? Or can't you say?"

"Can you keep it between just us?" I study Gary.

"Of course."

"My territory stretches between here, Portland, and California."

"Kind of broad. A promotion of some sort?"

"Yep. My immediate boss pushed me to apply. He's one of the few people I've told about my problem. It shocked me when the committee actually selected me."

"Why? You were first in your class at Quantico. And by the way, what was that like? I've never heard about your time there or what you did afterwards."

"Quantico was exciting. Twenty weeks of academic training, plus firearms and physical fitness. Then I served a year in Washington, five more years in Arlington. I thought about taking a leave of absence in between to check into my brother's death. Ended up only taking two weeks, and then came to Portland. "

"Did you find anything out."

"Not really."

"So this promotion's related to your new territory?"

"Kind of. I'm investigating industrial-sized cannabis operations in the Emerald Triangle. Humboldt, Trinity, and Mendocino counties in California, the Rogue Valley in Jackson, and Josephine County here. I'm heading up an entire unit."

"Our county?" Gary's mouth opens. "I didn't know we had a problem here. I know our people smoke pot once in a while, but grow it in distributor amounts?" Gary gets a dazed look.

"The problem's growing, and the FBI's new boss, wants us to make an example out of the biggest players."

"This is a big opportunity, Wayne. Who knows where it could lead, for you professionally. I still can't believe we have a problem in our county." It seems sad that somewhere we've both spent our childhood and where Gary is raising his children is now turning into a place where people will come to grow illegal drugs. Gary and I watch the rain drip down on the windshield. "Things like this could destroy our county, our way of life," Gary says, shaking his head.

"No doubt about that, but I'll do whatever I can to stop it. The only thing that worries me is my dyslexia. At my last job, I figured out workarounds. The Bureau never knew the full extent of the problem."

"Hell, Wayne, you can do that again," Gary says. "Hire a secretary. Have her do the heavy lifting. And I'll help you as much as I can, like you've always helped me."

I nod. "Yeah, maybe."

"Well, despite the thing that brings you here, it's nice to have you back." He shakes my hand. "Maybe a beer next time?"

"Of course. Congrats on the kids. I always thought you and Mary Ellen would be great parents."

"Believe me, a bar full of rowdy bikers is easy compared to three little girls." Gary gives me a wry smile, returns to his patrol car, and climbs back in. I watch him pull away and the rain falls harder. I'd like to confide in Gary and tell him it still takes me an hour or more to get through a page of written material. I can eventually figure it out if I have the time, but things haven't improved much for me since high school. I've just gotten better at hiding my problem from the world.

# 3
# excitable boy

<u>Wayne</u>

It's nine a.m. when I spot Gary's cruiser parked outside my motel. I tap on the passenger's side window. He unlocks the door, and I climb in. "I don't know how you feds always find a way to make the locals do your work for you," Gary laughs, passing me the file.

"You know that isn't true. This is personal." I take the file from his hand.

"Remember, you didn't get this from me," and Gary rubs his hands on his pants.

"How can I possibly forget when you won't let me? Let me take a look." I scan the first few pages inside my mother's folder. I only pick out a few words here and there. It's all a jumble. "Have you read this?"

"Yes." Gary rubs the back of his neck nervously.

"What were your thoughts, Gary?"

"Why are you asking me, Wayne?" And he leans towards me. "I'm a beat cop, not a detective."

"You know when something doesn't seem right, don't you?" I'm hoping he'll tell me what the report says, because I can't read much of this thing. I don't want to spend my whole evening figuring this out.

"I noticed the file was thin. And that the medical examiner said your mother's death is undetermined. What does that mean?"

"Like it sounds. There are five distinctions accepted in most states: natural, accidental, suicide, homicide and undetermined. Undetermined means it wasn't natural, but there isn't enough proof to say it was deliberate. I need to speak to the medical examiner to find out more. I may have to ask to exhume the body."

Gary shakes his head, "You think your pop's going to sign off on that?" Gary's voice disbelieving.

"I might not need his permission. As her son, if there's enough proof he did something, I can request it myself."

"You'd need evidence he's done something."

I nod. "So far, I haven't seen anything that gives me any proof that something suspicious occurred. I'll read the rest of this when I get back to my hotel room. Thank you for getting it for me." I'll probably spend the entire night deciphering it.

"How's the task force going?" Gary asks.

"I just started. This county is low on the totem pole. I'm putting the focus on California right now."

"And did you call Marnie?"

"Yes, but one of her sons answered. I'd go out there if I wasn't afraid of getting my head blown off, after all this talk about guns."

"If you want to meet Marnie, go to the diner. She works there," Gary says.

"She does?" I frown.

"Yeah, mornings and lunch."

"I was in there the other day. I never saw her, and Kate didn't mention it, even though it was her who gave me Marnie's number." I rub my chin. "You free for breakfast, Gary?"

"I am. You want to head over there?" Gary asks.

"Yeah. I could use some moral support when I ask her out."

"You sure you're ready for that?"

"No, but I have to try. I'm tired of one-nightstands. I had one a month ago. I met her in a bar where me and some of the other agents go after work. We both agreed before she invited me back to her place that it was strictly for sex. Then in the morning she gave me a hard time because I wouldn't exchange numbers or have breakfast."

"That's no fun."

"Nope. I've noticed that the most successful Bureau agents are grounded. They're either religious or committed to their family. They have something that keeps them together. The others drink too much, end up falling apart or eat their gun."

"Yeah, seen the same thing in my department. No sense taking two cars; we can go in my patrol car."

"A ride-along?"

"Not exactly. I'm not on duty." He gestures down at his civilian clothes. "Are you ready to meet the woman of your dreams again? I should give you a heads-up, dream girl carries."

"Kate told me."

"Did she tell you she hides a switchblade in her boot and an ax in her truck?"

"I'm glad she protects herself."

He snorts. "Uh-huh. Be careful, Wayne. It's impossible to predict how she might interpret your intentions."

"What do you mean? Marnie knows me." Gary pulls his cruiser out of the motel parking lot.

"She used to know you, Wayne. Carl, the diner's owner, has had to call us several times to quell a disturbance between a patron and her. I've heard there have been other times Carl's talked others out of calling the police by buying them off with free meals."

"Carl must be a good guy."

"He is. He understands Marnie better than she understands herself. It hasn't happened in a good number of years that I know of, but just be careful. Since her husband died, the wound may have been reopened."

"I will, Gary. For a cop, you have a lot of common sense and empathy." We circle the block searching for a parking spot. Ruby's is busy. Our second time around I point one out, "Over there, Gary," and he slides into a spot across the street from the place.

"We got lucky. She's lucky too," Gary says, stepping outside the patrol car.

"Shut up. Let's head over. I feel like two Peeping Toms standing out here."

MARNIE'S AT ANOTHER BOOTH, WAITING ON TWO TEENAGERS. SHE turns around to bring coffee to the new customers she's spotted, and by the time she realizes it's me in the booth, it's too late for her to stop. "Uh, um…ah, Wayne, you're back," she stammers, "Hi, Gary."

"Yep. Didn't Kate mention it?"

Marnie ignores the question. "Coffee?"

"Great, thanks," Gary says and nods his head.

Marnie's hand trembles, and her face turns red as she pours the coffee into my cup. She spills a few drops on the table. "Do you need time with the menu?" she asks.

"I'll take you," I manage to say, my voice betraying my nerves, as I tip the menu in Marnie's direction. Why did I say that? *I'm far more nervous than I anticipated.* She's more than lovely; she's a radiant presence, like an angel. Her hair, a golden shade of brown, is kissed by the sun's rays that stream through the window, creating a halo around her head.

A frightened expression appears in her eyes, disappears, and then changes to annoyance. "I'm not on the menu," she says. Marnie crosses her arms in front of her.

I keep talking. "I stopped in the other day and got your number from Kate. I called and left a message with one of your sons. I believe it was Cole. Perhaps he didn't give you the message, or maybe he did and you don't want to see me."

Suddenly a man in another booth says menacingly, "I told you to shut up, bitch." I turn and see a man yelling at a woman. The woman's face is pale, and she has a fading black eye.

"Excuse me a moment," I say, leave the table and take a few strides away from Marnie and Gary to the couple's table.

The man is still raising his voice at the woman when I arrive. "You do what I tell you to do."

"Is there a problem here?" I ask.

The man looks me up and down appraisingly, then stands, his face red. "Not yet. But if you keep poking your nose into business that isn't yours, there will be."

"Oh, but I think it is my business," I calmly reply, bringing out my wallet and flashing my badge as subtly as I can.

"Sorry, officer, I didn't know," the man grumbles.

"Not 'officer.' Special Agent. Now, next time I see her, I better not see any fresh bruises, you understand me?" I shouldn't have flashed my badge. That wasn't wise. I'm supposed to be on the down low. I should have let Gary handle it. I return to Gary and Marnie.

Marnie stares at me and glances back at the woman. "That's been going on for years. She'll never turn him in."

"Then she'll end up dead, like my mom."

Marnie's eyes water. "I regret not knowing your father abused her. I've always meant to tell you that."

"Most people didn't know. Who wants to tell other people what's going on in their home? I didn't even want my little brother to know."

"Did it happen a lot?"

"Not at first. Sometimes monthly, then weekly, and eventually nightly. It got to where neither of us invited friends over after school anymore."

"Why wouldn't your mother contact the police?"

"Because he was a cop. If she had turned him in, either the

police would've done nothing or he'd have lost his job. It was eventually the neighbors who informed on him, after seeing him beat Mark one day. I guess they finally drew the line at a man hitting a child."

"I remember that," Gary says. "His cop friends lectured him, but they never arrested him."

"That's right. Things calmed in the house for a while, but as they say, it was the calm before the storm. From then on, our house on Stone Barn Lane was a warzone, and I was the DMZ. I played peacemaker, or at least I tried. My father would hit my mother, my brother would hit my father, everyone would be bloody and worn out, and then things would cool down. You know, until they started up all over again."

"It's good that you and your brother did something, Wayne," Gary says.

"That's the thing, Gary. It was my brother who tried, but I let him down."

"How do you figure? You did all you could for both of them. Unless the victim presses charges, there isn't much anyone can do."

Marnie stares at me for a moment, then says, "I didn't get your message. That's why I didn't call you. Cole is...he doesn't appreciate anyone right now. He's difficult, like me."

"Well, then, how 'bout it, Marnie? Will you go out to dinner with me?"

"No, I'm not dating, right now." She pauses, then gives an awkward smile. "Meanwhile, what can I get you?"

"Just the coffee, thanks."

"Slice of apple pie, please and thank you," Gary says, pointing to the dessert case and smiling. Marnie walks away, and he turns to me. "Well, she didn't stab you. Good job." He puts his hand up for a high-five.

"Sorry to keep you hanging, but I'm not high-fiving until she calls me."

"Take my advice and meet her off-property, away from Cole.

The other one is fine, but the irony is that they're identical twins. Thank goodness they dress different."

"How bad can he be? He's only sixteen."

"Believe me, he's bad enough. He's been in juvie once already."

"For what?"

"Beating up another kid."

"How do you know he wasn't simply defending himself? Boys fight. Remember, we did our share."

"It's different with him. He's one of those kids who wears black all the time, and doesn't ever talk. I'd be scared to turn my back on him. But I'll tell you this, he listens to reason when she talks to him. Nothing and no one is ever going to get between them. Remember that, Wayne."

"I will, Gary. Thanks for the advice. Does he work?"

"Yeah, he does. Believe it or not, Grants Pass has a record store now. I know this'll come as a shock, but it turns out he hates working on a farm."

I RETURN TO MY ROOM AND PLOP DOWN IN THE ONLY CHAIR. I NEED out of this motel as soon as I can. It's beige everything except for the brown bedspread. The room is depressing. It makes me remember my past mistake. *I cheated on my SATs.*

I stare at the wall. My mind shifts to Cole. I know I can connect with him, because I know how it is not to fit in. I call my secretary, Janis, in Portland. "I know this is a weird request, but I need you to find out some of the bands moody teens who wear black all the time are into."

"You mean Goth bands?" Janis asks.

I pause. "What the hell are you talking about?"

"My nephew in Seattle is into all that. It's like punk rock, but… you know, sad and dark."

"Yeah, then I guess that's what I mean. And I need you to play some of the songs over the phone for me, too."

"You're kidding me, right?"

"I'm not. Help me out here."

She sighs. "Your perps are getting weirder and weirder." She hangs up.

An hour later, she calls me back. "Okay, so I got you some Siouxsie & The Banshees, The Cure, and Glori Mundi. Meanwhile, here's a song by a delightful group of gentlemen called Killing Joke."

The music starts playing, but after only a minute, I yell into the receiver, "Christ, turn it off. I can't take anymore."

"That's what I thought," Janis says, putting the phone back up to her mouth again.

"Great job, Janis. Thanks."

I wait until four before heading downtown. I find the store easily enough, called Rough Road Records, located one block off Main Street. I take my jacket and tie off, unbutton my shirt, run my hand through my hair and mess it up as best I can. It doesn't make me look younger but at least reduces my resemblance to a narc. I walk over and peer through the window at the album covers on display. A young teenage boy with bleached blonde hair and an angry expression is moving cardboard boxes about. That must be Cole.

The bell from the door is loud enough to be noticed when I push through it. Cole gives me a look that's more of a scowl. An album I actually recognize is playing, Warren Zevon's *Excitable Boy*. I pray this isn't a hint to what this kid is like. He gives me a good look up and down and says with a lot of skepticism in his voice, "Can I help you?"

"Yeah," I say as casually as I can. "I just got in from Portland and I'm bored with my music. I've been getting into some new stuff lately and was wondering what your selection is here."

Cole rushes over to me. "What have you been listening to?"

"You know, the usual—Siouxsie & The Banshees, The Cure,

Glori Mundi. I tried Killing Joke last week, but it was too harsh for me."

Cole's eyes light up, and he nods his head. "I know a brand-new band you'll like." He goes to the turntable, pulls an LP out of its sleeve, puts it on, and turns up the volume. "They're called Bauhaus, from England. They're my favorite right now. Listen to the guitar riffs; they're exceptional." He nods his head to the music. "This is an import, though, so it's kinda expensive."

"That's fine," I say. After it plays for a minute, I add, "The guy's vocals are haunting."

"You want haunting vocals, you should listen to Joy Division. You know them?"

"The name sounds familiar."

"Man, you need them." He pulls out a completely black album cover with a weird-looking illustration of topography lines on the front. "They're from England too."

"Can you give me that one on cassette so I can listen to it in my car?"

"Nah, these imports only come on vinyl. But…" He smiles and grabs a homemade cassette laying next to the cash register with the Joy Division album recorded on it. He hands it to me.

"Oh, I can't take your copy."

He shrugs. "I can make another one here whenever I want. Perks of the job." He gives a big grin.

"Well, I appreciate it. Thanks for your help, ah…"

"My name is Cole, Cole Tillman."

I put my hand on my chest. "Wayne Farr."

"Let me get you checked out." He takes both albums and slides them into a bag, ringing them up at the cash register. "I'm surprised someone so old is into this kind of music."

I laugh. "Thanks a lot."

"I didn't mean anything by it. Just, most people your age are into the Beatles and that other hippie bullshit. Even my mom says my music's creepy, and she's very open-minded."

"Of course it's creepy. That's why it's interesting."

"I wish everyone understood that." He shakes his head. "Anyway, that'll be twelve fifty for the two. Told you they were expensive."

I give him a twenty, and when he tries to give me change, I wave my hand. "Keep it. Consider it a finder's fee."

"Cole's eyes grow wide in shock. "Really?"

"Yeah. It's nice to not get made fun of, just for being an old guy who's into interesting music. Thank you."

"Come back anytime, Mr. Farr."

"Call me Wayne. By the way, do you happen to know of any places for rent in the neighborhood?"

"My friend's mom is renting a place. It's over on fifth Street. I'm not sure what the rent is, but there's a sign for it over there." He motions to a bulletin board near the front door, where I see a mimeographed flyer with little tabs at the bottom containing a phone number. I tear one off and head out.

I'm so preoccupied with my thoughts, I don't notice the woman crossing the street and making a beeline for me until she's right on me. "Hi, Wayne. What are you doing here?"

Crap, it's Marnie. "Oh, just purchasing some new music," I say as casually as I can.

"Oh yeah? What'd you get?" Before I can stop her, she pulls the bag out of my hands and starts rummaging through it. "Please don't tell me you're still into Elvis like in high school..." But her voice trails off as she examines the bag, holding up Cole's handwritten cassette. "Okay, what's going on?"

"Nothing. Like I said, I wanted some new music, and I just happened to meet Cole, who convinced me to try out some Goth bands. He seems like a nice kid."

"Nice huh? Don't give me that. No one, and I mean no one call's Cole nice. So, either you're out of your mind or you're trying to get in my pants and I can tell you right now you aren't getting into my pants. Don't think you're going to use my son to get closer to me. Is that what you're trying to do Wayne?" At this point Marnie's face is red and her eyes are mammoth. "Stay away from him, Wayne. You hear me?"

"But Marnie—"

She moves to slap me, and instinctively I reach out to stop her, accidentally pushing our bodies together through the force of the failed blow. Then before I know it. I'm planting my lips on hers. She struggles for a second. Her lips are moist and soft and then Marnie kisses me back. Electricity shoots through me. I'm surrounded by the scent of her, oranges and bacon and something more. It's like being in a time machine and I'm an eighteen-year-old kid again. Before I can say or do anything else, she turns and walks away, enters the record shop in a huff, leaving me on the sidewalk alone.

I want to chase her but return to my vehicle and sit instead. Lust from the kiss burns in my brain, and my fingers yearn to touch her. I'd love to march back to the record shop and push my tongue in her mouth, but that would not win any points after she told me to stay away. I need to get my mind off of Marnie. The manilla folder that holds my mother's crime report is on the seat. To distract myself from what just happened, I pick it up and flip through it again, but this time, I look at the crime photos at the end of the file instead of trying to decipher the words in the report. I stare at the position of my mother's body. One picture differs from all the others. It has a throw rug, pushed and bunched up near the edge of the cabinet that holds the sink. The other photographs don't contain the carpet. Where did it go? I need to find out.

I have to talk to him about it. My hands continue to shake as I rest them on the steering wheel. I rehearse what I'm going to say. I start the car and drive to my father's house as the sky darkens.

# 4

# the friendliest bank in town

<u>Marnie</u>

The bank last changed its decor twenty years ago. It still has the same grey carpets, wood paneling, and metal desks it did when my husband started doing business here. The clock on the wall say's 4:45. The bank closes in fifteen minutes.

The loan officer, Ed Loomis, is someone I've known since grade school. His desk is near the large safe in the rear of the building. There's no one waiting to see him, and no one's sitting in the chair by his station, providing the confidence for me to approach him. "Mr. Loomis," I begin, "Jack did business at this branch, and I was wondering if—"

"Jack has three outstanding loans," he interrupts, "and every one of them is in arrears. I couldn't grant you another one unless you catch up on these."

The calendar on the desk is one they give out for free every Christmas. I have one hanging on the wall in the kitchen at home. *The Friendliest Bank in Town*, it reads at the top of it. A bunch of liars is what they are. You can't believe what anyone says. "He's dead now. Perhaps you could see fit to put a new one in my name instead. It's 1978, after all. Women can get credit in their names now."

"I can't, Marnie. I wish I could." Ed removes his glasses, lays them on the baby-blue blotter on his desk, and rubs his eyes with the tips of his fingers. The frames are lightweight metal, bent in odd places, and the nosepiece is covered with tape. He reaches over, takes the application I'd picked up from his desk out of my hand, puts it in his desk drawer and closes it. He always was a chicken-shit. He won't even look me in the eye; or maybe he can't because he can't see me without his freakin' glasses.

"Come on, Ed. I have a gas credit card in my name. I've lived in this town all my life. I've banked here since I was twelve years old. I started with a passbook saving account so I could put my babysit-ting money somewhere, and you won't lend me the funds to help me save my farm?"

"Marnie, I can't. Your husband borrowed over four hundred thousand dollars. And with interest, it's growing every day."

"So even though I sat next to you through twelve years of school, and shared my answers with you in algebra so you could pass and go get your accounting degree, all that means nothing to you?"

"That's not how bank loans work, Marnie. It's nothing personal. Surely you can understand. This is how business is done."

I stare at him. He avoids making eye contact again. "I under-stand, all right," I finally reply. "I know why you work here now. You're a penny. Two-faced and not worth much."

His eyes drift to another man who's just entered. "Oh, Mr. Jenk-ins, so nice to see you again," Ed says, standing up. I jump up as well, and while Ed greets his new visitor, I slip his glasses from his desk into my pocket without him noticing, exit the bank, and walk back to my truck. I throw the glasses on the side of the curb as hard as I can, hear them crack, and climb in my vehicle. I roll the window up and down ten times before starting my truck and back up over the glasses. It's a childish move, but it makes me feel better. The deck is stacked against people like me.

I head over to my father-in-law, Frank Tillman's house. He's never liked me, and the feeling is mutual. He's one of those men who always has his hand out. He looks for ways to screw people, and now he's done it to me. I drive up to the small farm he runs with his other son, Jacob. It holds several greenhouses for which my husband and I paid for. He grows organic produce and sells to fancy restaurants in Portland. Frank's had it in for Jack ever since he inherited his grandfather's property, which Frank thought he had a right to. He used Jack's guilt against him to get him to lend him money or buy him things. Of course, Frank and Jacob disappeared when Jack got sick. They didn't stop by once to visit or help.

I knock on the door and wait for someone to answer. Frank's got a Pitbull chained up who's barking in his side yard. When no one comes to answer the door, I go check on him. His water bowl and food bowl are both empty. I find a hose, turn it on, fill the bowl, give it to him, and return to the door. I bang again and again, then switch to kicking it. After three minutes, Frank opens it. "Stop it, Marnie. You're making a racket. What do you want?" He scowls, his arms crossed in front of him.

"Jack loaned you money. I need it back."

"It was a gift," Frank smirks.

"Here's a tissue for that bullshit on your lip. Twenty thousand dollars is not a gift. I need it for taxes and to pay the loans to run the farm."

"Like I told you, Jack gave it to me. Sons help fathers."

"I can't believe you won't help your grandsons and the farm that's been in your family for generations."

"Don't try to guilt me into helping you."

"Excuse me? It's you who guilted your son into lending you money that it looks like you have no intention of paying back."

"Leave, Marnie, and don't come back. I don't like you."

Frank tries to close the door, but I've got my foot in it, preventing him. "You don't like me? That's a shame. I'll need a few minutes to recover from the tragedy. Just so you know, I've canceled the credit cards Jack gave you. I'm no longer responsible for any further charges in your son's name. If you use them, the authorities will arrest you." I pass him the letter I'd prepared and had notarized.

"What about my truck?" He asks and he reads the letter.

"It's not yours. It's in your son's and my name, Jack and Marnie Tillman. The vehicle needs to go back to the dealer."

"You can't make me."

"You're right. But the police can. I talked with the dealer, and he's agreed to transfer the loan in your name alone if you wish to go in and apply."

"You bitch." Frank's face turns tomato red, and he takes steps towards me like he wants to hit me. He used to beat his wife before she got fed up and walked out. I would see bruises on her when she came over for holiday dinners.

I simply shake my head in exasperation. "Turn your car in by tomorrow, or the police and the repo men will be out here to do it for you." I leave Frank fuming by the door, going down the steps and then the dirt path. I hop in my thirteen-year-old truck and sit there. I wish I could do something about the dog, but I didn't come for him, and Frank is watching me from the window. I start the truck, back out of the driveway, and head home. Life sucks when you can't even trust family. I warned Jack that he should have his father sign something when he lent him the money, but Jack refused to listen. "He's family," he had simply said.

I head towards my farm, pass Kate's blue Mitsubishi, and she waves me over to the side of the road. She rolls the window of her car down. "Did you decide?"

"About what?"

"Duh…the leftovers." She puts her hand over her eyes to keep out the sun.

Every door I tried was closed. My options are gone. I swallow. "Let's do it. Follow me to the reservoir and we can discuss the details."

Kate gets a wide smile. "I have to go somewhere first. Can we meet in half an hour?"

"How about an hour?"

She waves and nods, and I head for home. As soon as I pull in the drive, I see them. The snakeskins. They look like an aboriginal painting, squiggles of various sizes and even though translucent, you can see different patterns on them. The skins are everywhere, in pathways to the barn, in the fields by the cows, and even on the porch where I sit and read. As snakes grow, they shed their skin as often as once a month, although usually it's only a few times a year. This is the first time I've seen as many as this. I read once that the snake symbolizes transformation, death, and rebirth. It could be an omen. I gather the longer ones, bring them inside the house, and place them on my desk before returning and walking to the kennel to check on the dogs. Would changing into someone else be a good or bad thing?

I notice one of the boys has left several rocks on a table in the kennel. They know to keep their eyes peeled for rocks with interesting shapes I might want to paint. It's a hobby of mine. I collect them whenever I take walks, whether by the stream, a pond, or around the farm. After I paint them, I leave them around town for people to find. I've been doing it now for over five years. I know why I do the painting part—it's fun and creative—but I don't know why I feel compelled to drop them around town for people to discover. I don't even like most people, other than my children, the people I work with, and Kate. I know that's a terrible thing to say. Perhaps it's the only way I can connect with others, if you can call anonymously leaving rocks around "connecting."

My boys have watered and fed the dogs. I take Nova, another Pitbull mix, out of her kennel. She's white with chestnut spots. I put a lead on her, and she followed me to the truck. The dog jumps on the floor and then to the seat. She has hip problems and is standoffish. She doesn't bark much, only growls if excited. She's missing part of her ear, which makes her look scary, and one of the reasons I take her with me. Even though I don't need protection from Kate, the reservoir is secluded and dark, and you never know who you'll run into down there. I take an antihistamine tablet from my glove compartment and a gulp of water from my bottle on the seat, hoping to keep my allergy at bay.

I drive towards my destination, and a calm settles over me. Or is it an empty numbness? If I want to save the farm, I don't have a choice. No one is going to do it for me. You can't believe in anyone but yourself. I wrestle with my conscience. Selling drugs is wrong, but I stopped believing in right and wrong a long time ago, back when I was fifteen and the police department turned its back on my mother and me. My mother's unsolved crime is a folder that sits in a box, and her murderers are still out here somewhere.

As I approach the reservoir, I see Kate's blue Mitsubishi parked there, which is unusual. She's never on time for anything, ever. As I get closer, I see her standing outside her car. She looks gorgeous, as always. Her red hair is piled on top of her head with a clip. She's wearing a white crop top, bell-bottom jeans, and a black leather belt with a huge silver buckle. She's not alone; there's a man I've never seen before with her. He's tall and has dark brown hair pulled back in a ponytail, with a matching goatee. Like most of the men she goes with, this one is good-looking. Why did she bring a date when we need to discuss things?

I don't even want to get out of the truck, so I don't. I roll down the window halfway and roll it back up again, then repeat doing it twenty times. I park facing the water. It looks clean and pristine because it's a reservoir. You're not allowed to swim, boat or fish here. You can only admire it. The county protects it from people. That's a wise thing to do. People fuck everything up. There's a large black and yellow sign posted. It reads—*No Trespassing*.

Kate walks over to me and mouths, "Are you going to get out?"

"Who is he?" I point back at her accomplice. Kate knows I have trouble in new situations with people I've never met.

"A guy I know who's going to help us."

"You should've discussed it with me before bringing someone. Did I ask for help? I don't like surprises."

"We need a professional and he's safe. Let me introduce him to you."

"How do you know him?"

"I dated him a few times."

"Oh, great, one of your rejects."

"Can you say it louder? For God's sake, Marnie."

"What's his name?" I ask.

"Derek Live. He's from Merlin."

"So that makes him alright?"

"Yes. It's better if he's not from our immediate area."

"Why? Because he won't know I'm a nutjob?"

"Oh, no worries about that. I already warned him." Kate winks and goes over to the man, grabbing his arm as he leans against her car, smoking a cigarette. She drags him towards my truck and I climb down out of the cab, bringing Nova with me. I take several steps and Nova follows, staying close to me.

Derek comes forward, holds his hand out, and introduces himself, "I'm Derek. Marnie, right?" He notices the dog and bites his lips.

"Yep."

"Is the dog friendly?"

"As long as you don't make any quick moves."

Derek backs up, eyeing Nova. "Kate says you have some product you want to dump. I can help with that. What can you tell me?"

"What do you want to know?"

He turns to Kate. "I didn't come out here to waste my time. Does she want to sell or not?"

"Of course she does. Tell him the details, Marnie." Kate slaps my shoulder, making Nova growl.

"It's okay, Nova." I pat her head and turn to Derek. "I have seventeen pounds. It's good quality and clean. I took out the stalks, seeds, trash. It's almost completely buds."

"Do you think it's possible to put the dog in the truck? She's making me nervous." Derek takes another drag off his cigarette and stares down at Nova, then drops his cigarette on the ground and stomps it out, and Nova lifts her lip and snarls.

"Alright, if she's making you nervous." I walk Nova back to the truck and open the door. "Up, Nova." She hops into the floor of the truck with a grunt. I roll the window down to let in air and give her a way out. If I need help, I can call her. She'll just barely fit through the window.

Derek nods his head. "Thanks. What I'd like to do is sell a pound or more to people I trust. That way we don't call attention to ourselves and you ladies don't have to dirty your pretty little hands."

"My hands are already dirty. I grew the stuff." *What a condescending ass.*

"Point taken." He smirks. "What kind is it?"

"It's a good strain. The seeds are from Hawaii; it's a Sativa, Maui Wowie, a potent strain, thirteen percent THC."

"What's THC?" Kate asks.

"It's a mind-altering compound that can control your mood. It's what helped take the edge off of Jack's pain."

"How did you learn to grow?" Derek asks.

"I told you—" Kate answers.

"I didn't ask you, I asked her," he says, turning his back on Kate and pointing at me.

I roll my eyes at Kate. "I saw a pamphlet for sale in the back of a magazine at the beauty parlor where I get my hair trimmed, so I ordered it. It was a sleazy little thing, but it gave me the basics. I grew the plants from seed outside, late spring, through the summer last year. They got big, but I interspersed them with the corn on my farm and they blended in. I dried them in my barn."

"All of them made it?" A look of surprise spread across his face.

"Yes, I didn't lose any. My biggest one, Big Bertha, got bigger than the corn. I had to keep topping her. I ended taking her down early because I was afraid someone would notice. It broke my heart, but I didn't have a choice."

"You named them?" Derek laughs.

"Of course. They were like my children, and they were all different. Their growth spurts, the shape of their leaves, their coloring, even their buds."

"That's impressive for a beginner, not to lose any. Maybe because you're a farmer you notice things like pests and fungus."

"It had more to do with knowing I couldn't save my husband, so I put everything I had into growing the plants."

Derek nods his head. "Kate told me about your husband. Condolences. I'll move the product for you. And because you're an amiable lady, I'll only charge thirty-five percent."

"And if I wasn't, you'd take fifty? No thanks. Ten percent or you can walk."

"Stop trippin'." Derek shakes his head. "You think you can sell this by yourself and not get ripped off or end up in jail? Dream on, lady."

"I grew it by myself. I'm sure I can figure out how to sell it by myself if I have to. I mean, if you're doing it, how hard can it be?"

Derek's face tightens. "Alright, lady, I'll let you think on it." He swats the air, shakes his head back and forth, and stares at Kate.

I return to the truck, open the door, and make Nova move out of my seat as I climb in. Kate chases after me. "Come on, Marnie, selling is just as important as growing it. Do you really want to get involved with trying to move it by yourself? This guy is a professional."

"I'm not getting taken advantage of. Forget it." I turn the key in the ignition.

Derek walks over to my window and stands beside Kate. "Would twenty-five percent sit better, Marnie? You won't find anyone who knows what they're doing that will charge you less."

I frown, then nod my head in resignation. "Fine. I'm assuming you're going to push dime bags for ten dollars, like most people? Sell mine for twelve, because I know mine is better than anything else out there. That's..." I do the math in my head. " ...$1,536 retail per pound, so we should get around twelve-fifty back. You take your cut and give me an even thousand. And we always meet here.

Never call me or come to my house or my place of employment. Call Kate to arrange meetings. Do you agree?" Derek nods. "Call me when you've got a sale lined up and I'll get the product to you. "

As I drive away into the night, I see Kate standing next to Derek in my rearview mirror. He's smiling and nodding his head at me.

SINCE JACK PASSED AWAY, IT'S BEEN A CHALLENGE TO SLEEP ALONE. A warm dog would do nicely if I wasn't allergic. What would people think of a grown woman who sleeps with a teddy bear? Next to my nightstand is my rifle. People would have an easier time picturing me with that.

I didn't realize then, but starting on that day, May 2, 1978, nothing in my life would be the same; and that could only be a good thing. I'd just negotiated my first drug deal. I'm proud, yet frightened. What's going to happen next? I lay in bed and obsess all night about what actions to take; How to beef up security, the weapons I need to keep handy, and which guns I haven't cleaned lately. I finally fall asleep hours later.

*"What would you like to drink?" the flight attendant asks? I don't answer right away. I'm sitting in first class, and when I glance out the window, I see soft clouds and a light blue sky.*

*"Champagne, please." She'll have some, too, and I point to Kate sitting next to me.*

*"Where are we going?" Kate asks.*

*"We're going shopping in Paris. I must spend some of the money I'm making. Suddenly, Kate's gone, and I'm no longer on the plane. Wayne is dressed in a black tuxedo, and we're on a dance floor. "You shouldn't be here." He either ignores me or can't hear me. He takes me in his arms and smiles. I'm wearing a turquoise dress; the neckline is round, the sleeves are flounced, and I look pretty for once; my hair is styled on top of my head,*

*and I've applied make-up. Wayne kisses me long and deep. He takes my hands and pretends to dance with me.*

*"I'll protect you," Wayne says. What will he protect me from, getting my foot stepped on? Suddenly, an alarm goes off, and out of nowhere, police come from all directions and arrest me. I notice my sons are watching. I've been arrested in front of my sons.*

I open my eyes, lift my head, stare at my clock, and realize it's just my alarm going off. I check the time. 6 am. The whole thing was a nightmare. I don't have time to go back to sleep. I climb from my bed, exhausted, and prepare for work at Ruby's.

# 5
# hotwired

<u>**Wayne**</u>

I knock on the front door several times. He's got to be home. It's dinner time. Footsteps shuffling towards the door and finally it creaks open. "Wayne, you're home. Did you bring your brother?" His eyes cloud with confusion.

"No, Pop. Remember, Mark passed. Can I come in?"

"Is Mom gone, too?" He opens the door wider, scratches his head.

"Yes, Pop. I'm hoping you can tell me what happened to her."

He shrugs, "Um, I don't know." His voice grows softer, and he motions for me to follow. We sit down in the living room, and my father continues. "She went to make dinner. There was a loud crash, but I didn't go out and check because the UD game was on and a pick six had occurred. You know your mother dropped things all the time."

"What happened after that?"

"It was halftime, and I was hungry. I called your mother to bring me a beer and something to eat. She didn't come. I yelled out and she still didn't come. I went myself to get the beer and found her. I called an ambulance because I couldn't wake her, but by the time they arrived, she was gone. She was..." His voice drifted away, and his eyes lock on the bear head and grow distant.

"Let me show you something." I pull the photograph from the folder and point at the rug scrunched up by the sink in the photo. "Do you think she slipped on the throw rug?"

"I don't know. I don't have them anymore. The police never asked about them," and he frowns.

He should have checked on her when he heard the crash, but it's too late for a lecture. "Do you want me to fix you dinner, Pop?"

"Sure, Wayne."

I make cheese omelets, and we eat them in the living room in front of the television. The evening news discuss NASA's selected its first women astronauts: Sally K. Ride, Shannon W. Lucid, Margaret Rhea Seddon, Kathryn D. Sullivan, Judith A. Resnik, and Anna L. Fisher.

My father shakes his head. "Why do we need women astronauts?"

"Why shouldn't they go into space? They have certain advantages."

My father scowls and ask, "Like what?"

"Women take up less space, they're more agile, have a better sense of smell, they listen better, are better communicators, and I've heard their layer of fat makes them better at handling cooler temperatures. That's just a start."

"Where do you get all this, Wayne?" He shakes his head.

"I heard it somewhere."

After we're done, I put the dishes in the dishwasher and head back to my motel. As I drive, I decide that most likely the only thing my father is guilty of, besides being a bad father, is being a lousy husband. A throw rug was the culprit in my mother's death, and my father didn't call for help in a timely way. It was most likely an accident.

**<u>Marnie</u>**

"We had a deal, Derek. You aren't supposed to be here." I refuse to look at him. I glance around the rest of Ruby's to see if anyone is watching us. He just proved he's not someone I can trust.

"Take a chill pill, Marnie. Sit down and we can talk about it."

"Are you always this stupid, Derek, or is this a special occasion? If you haven't noticed, I'm working. We had an agreement." Inside my mind, I've killed him ten times, in ten different ways.

"Come on, lighten up."

"I told you the rules," I whisper. "You can't show up where I work. What if my boss finds out what I'm doing? He's cooking and can see and hear through the window from the back." I point in that direction.

"The only way he'll find out is if you keep freakin' out about it." Derek tilts his head and squints.

"If you ran your body like you ran your mouth, you'd be Charles Atlas. Order something, Derek, or get out." I glance at other tables to see if people are listening. So far, the mother in back of us is distracted, yelling at her children to stop pouring salt from the shaker all over the table. I check the booth next to us where two senior citizens are staring at the menu. One of them is wearing hearing aids.

"Fine. A cheeseburger, fries, and iced tea with plenty of sugar."

"How do you want that cooked?"

"Rare."

I hand the ticket to Carl, where I've written "CB kill it," and fetch Derek's drink. I bring it back and point to the sugar. "Add your own. Carl only makes plain."

Minutes later, Carl shouts, "Order up."

I present Derek's food. "Anything else?"

"Tonight at the reservoir, at five," Derek says.

"Too early. I have kids. Make it seven. Eat that and leave." I slap the bill on the table.

"I have to say, your customer service leaves much to be desired, Marnie."

"Isn't there a car you could jump in front of?"

"Do you always have to be so sarcastic?"

"Sarcasm comes out of my mouth like stupid falls from yours. Now get out."

"I hope you aren't expecting a tip."

"I'll give you one, Derek. You see that door? I want you on the other side of it."

He shakes his head, picks up the check, and heads to the register. Wait until I tell Kate that Derek came to the diner. I am not meeting him at the reservoir by myself. I walk to the phone in the back of the restaurant and phone Kate. She answers right away. "Are you feeling better?"

"A little," Kate says.

"You won't believe what Derek did. He came to the diner."

"Why?"

"How the hell do I know? I didn't discuss it with him. I thought you said he was safe."

"Hmm. I thought he'd be okay."

"He wants to meet tonight at the reservoir. I'm not going alone."

"I've got a date."

"I thought you're sick."

"I'll be well by then."

"What time are you going out?"

"Seven-thirty."

"We're meeting at seven. You should be there. Go to your date afterwards. You can be a few minutes late."

"Alright, if you insist."

"Kate, help me straighten him out or I'm pulling the plug."

"You can't. Derek could blow the whistle on us. He knows too much. It's best we follow through."

"Your logic makes no sense," I say.

"It could be you're paranoid where he's concerned," Kate says, "And overreacting."

"Do you think I am?"

"A little. Why don't we listen to what Derek says first before making any decision."

"Are you saying I'm too worked up about a guy who refuses to do something he agreed to? Didn't he agree not to call? Him coming to the diner was wrong."

"I agree with you, but let's hear him out first."

"Alright, I'll do what you say. Where were you today?"

"You already know where I was—I didn't feel well. Don't you believe me? I'm sick."

"Of course I do. I'd trust you with my life." The truth is, it's impossible to trust anyone; Kate's as close as I get to trusting anyone besides my children.

I hang up the phone and walk through the kitchen. "You going to wait on people or do I have to hire another server?" Carl barks.

"Keep your britches on. Last time I checked, everyone was served." I push through the swinging doors, glance around the restaurant, and notice two Grants Pass police officers have just taken their seats in a booth. I become nervous.

"Are you going to serve them?" Carl points.

"Of course." I grab coffee and menus. "Hello, Joel, Eddie. Coffee?"

"Hi, Marnie." Both nod but neither one looks at me, but I'm used to it. Most of the cops don't. They're either embarrassed because they've never solved my mother's murder, or because they don't like my son Cole, or they're tired of dealing with my meltdowns; I don't care which one it is. Unlike many of the people of Grants Pass, I have little respect for the police in this town. How could I when they've never found the men who murdered my mother? I bring water, menus, and napkins and eavesdrop on them while I do.

"Yeah, so directives came down from the higher-ups to be on the lookout for strangers moving into GP that might be growing marijuana," Eddie says. "Can you believe it? In our little town? This could become a big thing, like in California."

"It must be because of our soil and out-of-the-way location," Joel says.

"The FBI is getting involved, too. They're going to do fly-bys eventually. I don't know when." Eddie spreads his palms before him.

"Should I give you time to decide?" I ask.

"No, afternoon breakfast for us," Eddie nods. "Eggs over easy, hash browns, sausage, and white toast. Thanks, Marnie."

"I'll have pancakes, thank you." Joel hands me his menu. "Did you hear they spotted a gigantic black bear over on Jenkins Farm?" he says to the others.

"I heard it turned out to be Mrs. Jenkins in a fur coat," Eddie says. The men all laugh.

"Make those eggs medium for Eddie or he'll send them back," I say passing the slip to Carl.

"I have that guy's number. They should arrest him." Carl laughs.

As my shift ends at three and I'm heading for the door, I recognize the sales associate, Bill, from the Chevrolet dealership entering. He asks, "Marnie, that truck we discussed. You bringing it back?"

"I'll try."

"The finance manager is riding me. If you don't want a big hit on your credit report, you need to bring it in or bring the payments up to date."

"My father-in-law has possession, and he's giving me static."

"You don't have a key?"

"No."

"We can have another one made. It'll cost you a hundred and fifty bucks, but it's better than having a repo on your record."

"How can I get the key from him if I can't even get the truck?"

"Find someone who's good at hotwiring cars. If you have a copy of the title, a cop wouldn't stop you."

"I have the paperwork; you guys hold the title. "

"Of course. If you need a good repo man, call me. But they'll charge you too," Bill says.

As I climb into the truck headed for home, I sense my world crumbling. If I have a repossession on my credit report, it'll be there for seven years; but if I need the truck hotwired, I'll need money to pay for it. I have damn Derek Live to deal with too. Coming to my place of employment when I told him not to. I slap the steering wheel. I have nothing, and people are trying to take away even that.

I pull in my drive too fast and press my brake pedal hard, making gravel shoot everywhere. My son Chester sits on the porch swing, strumming his guitar. I jump out of the truck and tramp up the steps. "Whoa, Momma, you pulled in here like Speed Racer," he says, laughing. "And what did you do to your hair? It looks like you put your finger in an electric socket." I glance in the window of the front door. He doesn't exaggerate.

Cole walks out of the house. "What are we having for dinner? What's wrong with your hair?"

"Meatloaf and baked potatoes." I ignore the hair comment.

"Sounds good," they say in unison.

"Are the animals fed?"

"Yep, all of them," Chester says.

"The dogs too?"

"Yes, and a lady came by and dropped off another one. It's in good shape, but we're out of runs. I put the new one in with Nova."

"Did you treat her for worms and fleas?"

"Yes, Mom. How are we going to feed them? We're running low on dog food."

"Carl donated venison from a deer he killed. It's in the freezer at work."

"That's cool," Cole says. "I should put a few signs up on the bulletin board at the record shop. Some of these guys are adoptable. They deserve homes."

"I agree. Do it and I'll hang some at the grocery store."

"We won't have room to take others if we don't find people to take them."

"You're right, Cole. I couldn't keep doing this without you two helping me."

Chester puts the guitar down and comes toward Cole and me. We hug each other with the sun going down, putting on a show for us. The farm hasn't looked this beautiful to me in years. I remind myself that I'm doing this to save it for them.

I enter the house and make dinner, and we sit and share our day. Cole is happier than I've seen him in a long time. It made his day, waiting on Wayne in the record store and helping him buy that music he likes. I won't ruin it for him and tell him Wayne was trying to win favor with me.

At 6:45, while the boys clean up, I find the papers for my father-in-law's truck and put them in my purse. I tell my sons I'm meeting Kate, climb in my bucket of bolts, and head for the reservoir. Of course, Kate isn't there when I arrive, but Derek Live is. How he gets around without a vehicle, I'll never know. I stay in the truck with the doors locked. He must find it funny, because he has a big smile on his face as he strolls over and motions for me to roll it down. I do, a quarter of the way. "You're not getting out?" Derek asks.

I look in the rearview mirror and see Kate's Mitsubishi coming down the road like a bat out of hell. "Of course I am," and swing the driver's door open fast and hard, hitting Derek on purpose.

"Ouch, that hurt. What's your problem?"

"I was about to ask you the same thing. We had a deal. You weren't to come to my place of employment or to my home, or to call them either. You're to do everything through Kate, but then you show up at the diner, wanting to talk to me. What's that about?"

"It's a free country the last time I checked. Are you telling me I can't go to the only place in town to grab a bite to eat?"

"Yes, that's what I'm telling you. If you don't like that, we don't have to do business."

"Listen, I came to tell you I had someone who wanted to purchase five pounds, but they wanted a discount of $800.00 per pound in return for the bulk buy. He wanted an answer today, but because of your little hissy fit at the diner, I couldn't give him one. Talking this out through Kate and doing business at the reservoir slows things up. Don't you understand?" He pokes my chest with his finger.

"Don't put your hands on me," I reply angrily. "If you do it again, I'll—"

Kate comes between us. "Everyone calm down. I'm sure we can come up with an arrangement that works for everybody."

"No we can't," I say. "Not unless he does something to make up for the rules he's already broken."

"What are you talking about?" Derek scrunches up his face.

"You're going to have to earn my trust back."

"Jesus Christ, lady, you're too much. Who do you think you are, Michael Corleone?" Derek chuckles. "Just for kicks, what is this thing I have to do?"

"I need you to hotwire a truck and take it to the Chevrolet dealer in town."

"I'm already breaking one law. Now you want me to boost cars too?"

"It's just one truck, and it's mine, currently in possession of my dick of a father-in-law. He has the key and won't give it to me, but I have the paperwork right here."

"So the guy is likely to shoot at me?"

"Possibly."

"You're a piece of work, Marnie."

"I have to go," Kate says. "You two work it out, but don't kill each other. We'll talk tomorrow. Kisses." She hops in her car, speeding away, and not glancing back.

"Alright, take me to your father-in-law's," he says. "And do me a favor. Don't take your gun out. I've heard about you. If I'm going to be shot at, I'd prefer to know which direction the bullets are coming from."

"Fine. Do you know how to hotwire a vehicle?"

"Sure. It's easy. Does your father-in-law own any dogs?"

"Yes, a Pitbull."

"Shit. What is it with farmers and Pitbull's in this town?"

"Don't worry, he's in a pen."

Once I'm near Frank's farm, I pull off the main road. "You stay here. I'll see if the truck is there." I walk into the woods and come up behind the house. The truck isn't there, but the dog is barking his head off. Frank must be somewhere else. The house is dark, which likely means his son Jacob is out, too. I circle the dog pen and find the pitty chained. He stops barking as soon as I come near. I unlock the pen, enter, and examine the water bowl—empty again. I take the bowl, find the hose, fill it, bring it back to the dog, let him drink and get his fill. When he's done, I unchain the dog, take my belt off, thread it through its collar, and lead him back to my truck. "Come on, boy," I say, and he jumps in, seeming happy to leave his present owner.

"You're stealing his dog too?" Derek asks. "You're something else."

"My father-in-law doesn't deserve to own him. If he wants the dog back, he can come find me, but he won't, because he doesn't give a damn about it."

"I'm not seeing any truck."

"Yeah, he must be out with it. We can check out a couple of places he goes. I'm sure he'll be at one of them."

"You know best," Derek says.

We hit pay dirt at Jack and Jill's. The best part is that Frank had to park the truck in the back lot because of overcrowding, and the back lot isn't lit. Derek wasn't kidding; it isn't hard to hot-wire a car, or else he's an expert. Derek has it started in less than a minute.

After I follow him to the dealer, Derek parks the Silverado and walks up to my truck. "You want the keys?" He holds them in the air like a trophy.

"Where did you find them?"

"Under the seat," he smirks.

"They need to go in the drop box."

"So do you finally trust me now?" Derek asks.

"That's still up in the air." Derek turns and I watch him put the keys in the dealer's metal box. He returns to the truck and climbs back in.

"What did you decide to do about the five pounds at eight hundred?"

"A thousand is as low as I want to go. I can always sell it myself, so he's not doing me any favors."

"I think I can sell him on that. When can I pick it up?"

"Tomorrow night, but at the reservoir. No more coming by my work again."

"So, I can't just swing by your house right now?"

"No. We've established how this works." We sit in silence, a minute passes, Derek seems to accept it and doesn't run his mouth, trying to convince me otherwise. I don't have to say something sarcastic to shut him up. He helped me handle a looming problem getting my father-in-law's truck back, but before I can think further or thank him—

Derek gives a fake yawn and flops one arm over my shoulder, and winks at me. "Perhaps I can change things," then leans further over and tries to kiss me.

I push him away. "Do you have a death wish?"

Derek smirks. "It must be tough without a husband."

"It's not tough at all. Men are expendable. Now leave my vehicle, please."

He climbs down out of the truck and I slowly start pulling away. He jogs along the side of the car. "You gotta be kidding. You're leaving me here? How am I going to get home?"

"You're a resourceful guy. I'm sure you'll figure out something."

He calls after me, "What time tomorrow?"

"The same." I look in my rearview mirror and see him standing in the middle of the road. I'm proud of myself for dumping him like that. I shouldn't have been.

I stop at the phone booth near the grocery store and call Wayne's pager. He calls me right back. "I'm surprised, Marnie. I figure I didn't have a snowball's chance in hell of hearing from you. Where are you?" Wayne voice makes me feel warm inside, like someone cares.

"The phone booth near Ruby's."

"Do you want to meet at my motel?"

"Good girls don't come to men's hotel rooms."

"Pretend you're not a good girl. Or I can come to you. You decide."

"Hmm. You're making things difficult." I pause. "I'll be over soon, but I'm warning you, I'm only staying a while. It's a school night, and I have a dog with me." I hang up the phone.

A few minutes later, I pull into the motel's parking lot. Wayne is standing in front of the motel's lobby, waiting. "I didn't expect you to be out here," I say.

"What kind of gentleman would I be not to greet you? Should we go in?"

"Let's stay in the truck."

"Hit and run?" Wayne asks with a smile.

"I guess."

"It's so good to see you again, Marnie." Wayne pats the dog's head, then scoots it out of the way, making it take the window seat. He takes my hand. I'd forgotten how large they are. His fingers are warm, and his pulse beats with mine. I move closer to him and lean my head against his shoulder. The motel sign blinks above us—*vacancy, vacancy, vacancy.*

It's been almost three months since Jack died, but the truth is, he left me years before that. I can't say I'm sorry he's dead. He suffered badly the final year, and I didn't want that for him. Our marriage wasn't perfect, and I never loved him in that all-consuming way, but the worst part was that I'd stopped respecting him. Jack had driven the farm into the ground, put us into debt, and stopped contributing long before his illness. He kept forcing me to do more and more. Still, I'd never wanted him to suffer. I'd liked him well enough to marry him, and it suited me back then.

The simple truth is that I didn't need or want love after my mother's rape and murder. Jack gave me two sons who I adore, Chester and Cole. I'll always be grateful for that. After I gave the other child away, I worried God was going to punish me. Having Chester and Cole helped me heal and gave me hope for the future. But when Jack got sick, Cole started acting out, and since then it's been downhill for him. I understand. I've never fit in here, either. Wayne is the only one who understood me, and I pushed him away, but now he's back. I wonder if we can make it work this time.

I don't wait for Wayne this time. I claim his mouth with mine and each kiss becomes more savage. I erase the past with each one. Each kiss becomes hotter, further consumes my sadness, and makes the world disappear. My breath touches his ear.

Wayne sighs. "You're killing me, Marnie." I bring my hand to Wayne's pants and his erection. It throbs through the fabric, straining to break free. I unzip his pants, put my hand into his underwear, and stroke him. His cock is warm and grows harder and more significant in my hand until the dog jumps on top of Wayne's lap and lays down. "I guess that's the end of that," Wayne says, chuckling.

# 6

# money back guarantee

<u>Marnie</u>

I experience a blend of emotions as I tuck one-pound packages of weed into my tote bag. I check all the locks on the windows and proceed towards the door. "Going out again?" Chester's head tilts to one side.

"The library has a couple of books ready for me to pick up." I slip on my windbreaker.

"I've never seen you go out so much, but you deserve to, with what went on with Dad." Chester rubs his chin and his eyes shine with pity.

I feel guilty lying to my son, so I change the subject. "Where did your brother go?"

"I'm not sure. How long are you going to be?"

"What are you, my father?"

"I wish I were. I'd ground you." A small smile builds and reaches his eyes. Chester looks more like his father every day.

"I'll be home in an hour or two." I hoist the bag's strap over my shoulder.

"You better be, young lady, or you'll lose privileges," Chester teases. "Can you bring back ice cream?"

"What kind?"

"Mint chocolate chip."

"Alright, but you are aware Cole doesn't like that kind?"

"Yes. You can buy him that gross coffee flavor he likes."

"We'll see." I head for the door. I make sure I have the knife in my boot and the bear spray in my pocket, then reach for the gun in the glove compartment and put that in my jean jacket. No way am I going to this meeting unarmed. "Self-defense" is a lie; you're either predator or prey, and there's no way I'll ever be prey again. You have to go into any meeting with that attitude. I considered taking a dog, but my sons would've asked too many questions. The sun has already disappeared behind the trees, and the sky is streaked with pink and orange, as I back out and head down the drive. I consider all the events that might occur during the sale and what I'll do about it, playing them repeatedly in my mind.

The empty road toward the reservoir gives me a reason to daydream until an animal streaks in front of the truck. Is it a raccoon or a possum? No, wait, it's a dog. I braked, but it was too late, and I hit it. It bounces over the hood and onto the roadside. I bring the vehicle to the side of the road, stop, exit the truck, and walk back, searching for its body. He has one eye open, and it looks like a giant black pearl…the dog has cataracts. That's why he's on the road; his sight's impaired. Someone's abandoned him. That's what people do with old animals they don't want to care for anymore. His muzzle is grey, and part of the dog's head and chest are crushed; even if I take him to my vet, he won't make it. But I can't leave him here to suffer.

I take the gun out of my jacket. My hand is shaking, but it doesn't stop me. I shoot him once in the head and then again, as tears flood my eyes. I take his back legs and drag him further off the road. I return to my truck and climb back in. My stomach churns and my heart aches. If I hadn't been driving at such a high rate of speed and preoccupied with other thoughts, I would've had time to avoid hitting him. I could've rescued him and taken him home; his last month's could've been happy ones. I bury my head on the steering wheel and cry some more. My hands are still shaking. "I don't have time for this." After a minute or two, I pull myself together, place the key in the ignition, start the truck, and proceed to my destination. I push it all out of my mind, pretending that none of it bothers me.

As I pull closer to where we're supposed to meet, I see Derek, but the vehicle he's leaning against causes me to do a double-take. I can't believe what I'm seeing. My hands grip the wheel tighter and anger floods through me, causing my face to heat and my foot to push the accelerator to the floor. Derek's got his hands on the door of my father-in-law's Silverado, which we stole from the bar and left on the dealer's lot last night. I distinctly remember seeing Derek drop the keys in the dropbox myself, so did he Hotwire it to steal it?

I pull into the parking area and brake hard, because if I don't I'll hit him. Dirt and rocks fly up and hit Derek. He jumps out of the way. "Shit," he calls out, seeming to duck for cover, losing his smile. "What's your problem?" he screeches.

"What's yours?" I yell back, jumping out of my truck and approaching him, shaking my finger. "What are you doing with this?" I motion towards the truck.

"What's the big deal? I borrowed it back." Derek spreads his palms before him. "You left me stranded with no ride. What was I supposed to do, walk ten miles at night?"

"Are you aware of the predicament you've placed me in by removing that from the dealer's lot? They'll destroy my credit."

"They'd need to repossess it for that to occur. You can follow me to the dealer tonight. We can drop it off and you can drive me to where I'm staying. Then everything will be hunky-dory."

"I'm not driving you anywhere unless you're dead, your body's in my truck's bed, and I'm on the way to bury you, you asshole."

"If you don't, I'll need to rely on this right here." Derek slaps the driver's door with the palm of his hand.

Luckily, Kate arrives and exits her car before I jump onto Derek. She shakes her head. "Can't you two ever stop fighting?"

"He's a moron."

No sooner do my words leave my mouth than a white Cadillac pulls in beside us. I can see the silhouettes of four men inside. The driver and the person on the passenger's side open their doors and climb out. Music from the car drifts outside as they walk towards us. "Where's the goods?" a man with his hair styled in a shag haircut asks. He's tall and olive-skinned.

Derek glares at him. "Cash first, then you see the product."

The man with the shag haircut turns to the other man, the driver. "Get the money." The driver, a shorter man with a bowl haircut in the front but long in the back, takes a couple steps to the car, returns with a brown paper bag, and passes it to his colleague. He opens the bag, glances inside, and allows Derek to inspect its contents. "It's all there, six thousand two-hundred fifty dollars, the amount we agreed on. Now I want to see the pot."

Derek looks at me. I walk to my vehicle, open the door, reach underneath the seat, grab my tote, walk back, and pass it to him. He looks in, smiles, and lets the man with the shag smell the bag. "It smells good," the man says. "Will it smoke as well? We smoke some."

"This is the same stuff you've already sampled." I clutch my jacket to my body, feeling for my gun.

"Alright, we weigh them first. Get the scales," he says to the other man.

"You think I don't know what I'm doing? Every pound is right on the money." Derek subtly shakes his head at me, as if to warn me not to start any shit with them. I shrug my shoulders in return.

"We will see," the man with the shag haircut says, walking towards my father-in-law's truck and placing the scale on the hood. "Give me one," he motions to Derek. Derek passes the man one of my prepared packages of pot. I hold my breath as the man pops it on the scale. Unless their scale is faulty, it should show sixteen ounces. "Good," the man says as the scale hits the sixteen-ounce mark. He repeats the process with each one and says to his colleague, "Give them the money."

"Count it," I say to Derek when they throw him the paper bag. "And check for any marked, counterfeit, or torn bills."

"What?" the man with the shag says, giving me a shocked expression.

"It won't be any use to me if it's not legal tender."

The man shakes his head and waits as Derek examines the money. "It's all good," Derek says after several minutes.

"We do business again?" the man with the shag asks.

I nod and watch them head back to their Cadillac with their scale and the marijuana. "Stop!" I put my hand in the air

The two men freeze, and the one with the shag turns around," Yes?"

"May I have my tote back? It's good for transporting product."

The men laugh and shake their heads. The one with the shag says to his driver, "Put the dope in the trunk and bring her bag back." After the man did so, he handed my bag to me. "We good now?"

"Thank you. Oh, wait a minute." I hold up my hand, go over to my truck, reach under the passenger's seat, and find my bag of rock art. I paw through it, find the one I'm searching for, bring it over, and pass it to him.

He raises his eyebrows and gazes with delight at the rock that no longer looks like one. "A pink Cadillac," he exclaims. "Did you make this?" I nod my head. "I love it. Thank you." He displays a wide grin, then punches his friend on the arm and shows it to him with a smile. The two men return to their Cadillac, wave, and drive away.

Derek takes a long, loud exhale. "That was fantastic. You know, except for almost getting us killed over a purse."

"It's not a purse. It works well for transporting the dope, and it's easy to slide under the truck seat. Why should I have to buy a new bag every time I need to transport the pot? Now hand over my cash."

"Our cash," Derek says. "And you've never painted a rock for me."

"My cash. Hand it over, and I'll give you what you're owed." Derek hands me the paper bag. I owe him $1,250 but it's all in twenties, so I count out $1,260 instead and give it to him.

Derek shakes his head. "An extra ten bucks. Thanks for your generosity."

"You did your job. I don't have change." I walk to my truck and I motion for Derek to follow me. "I brought three more pounds with me and I'm giving them to you upfront. Sell them, bring me the money, and you get three more." Derek nods and I reach under the seat and slide out the pot. "Remember, don't give it to people without them paying first."

"Seems like you have this whole thing figured out."

"I don't, Derek, but I'm not getting taken advantage of, by you or anyone else. That's been happening all my life. Now get in that truck and drive it to the dealership. And this time you're going to leave it there."

"Not without a ride."

Kate comes nearer and whispers, "Why do you have to be so mean? Would it kill you to give him a ride?"

"It very well might." What if he lives somewhere where no one could hear me cry for help? What if I couldn't get to my weapon fast enough? What if he overpowered me?

Kate reads my face, pats my arm, and makes eye contact. "I'll follow you both to the dealership, then I'll give him a ride wherever he wants to go, and you can go home. How's that sound?"

I wasn't about to leave my best friend alone with Derek Live. "We'll both give him a ride to where he wants to go." And we do. We drop Derek off at Jack and Jill's.

"Trust is difficult for you, I understand," Kate says as we sit in my truck in the parking lot.

"I've got two reasons I don't trust people, Kate," and I drive away from Jack and Jill's parking lot. "Number one, I don't know them. Number two, I know them. With someone like Derek, he's already demonstrated I can't. You heard what he did, coming to Ruby's and then saw what he did, stealing my father-in-law's truck, back from me."

"I understand."

"Do you, Kate?"

"Yes. Your past, the home invasion, your mother's murder."

"It isn't just that. When you grew up poor like I did, eating cereal with water instead of milk tastes fine. Washing my underwear in the sink seemed normal. Sometimes my bestie gave me some of her clothes she hadn't worn, with the tags still on them. Do you know who she was?" Kate looks silently down at her lap, because she knows I'm talking about her. "So now you know how it is, and why I don't enjoy being with people I don't know. Why I have a hard time trusting anyone, or fitting in and getting along with others. I can't allow myself to be ripped off by someone like him."

"It's going to be alright. You're not your mom. You'll sell the rest of the pot, you'll get your money, and you'll pay the tax bill. Derek Live won't get the better of you," Kate says, and I pull into the lot of the grocery store.

"I'm sorry. I'm freaking out and whining."

"You should do it more. I'm not strong enough to have gotten through what you did." Kate's voice is soothing. We're sitting side by side in a dark car in the parking lot. For the first time all night, I'm not driving somewhere or having to worry about someone ripping me off. The lights from the parking lot don't reflect on the truck. I realize I should have parked closer. I start the truck and move it to a spot by the entrance under a light where it's safer.

"I hit an elderly dog on the way over to the drop. He reminded me of Whiskers," I tell Kate.

"Oh, Marnie. I'm so sorry." She hugs me.

I pull away. "I had to finish him off. It tore my heart out to shoot him, but I couldn't let him suffer. It brought everything back. It hit me like a train. I'm sorry I'm dumping on you. I should stop."

"It's alright. You can. You know that."

"I promised Chester some ice cream. Will you come in with me? Do you mind?"

"Sounds good. I could go for some strawberry." Kate runs her tongue across her lips. "Ice cream always makes things better."

"Does that come with a guarantee?"

"Money-back, Marnie," Kate says, and she drapes her arm around my shoulder and squeezes. She's the only friend I've got. I hold back my tears, thankful I have someone in my life I can talk to. The neon sign at Gloria's Supermarket, blood red on a white background, flashes at me. I think about the dog I shot tonight, the blood and memories of Whiskers too, while Kate and I walk into the store together. I pass people pushing shopping carts and wonder if their lives are as sad as mine.

# 7

# promises

<u>Dan</u>

**D**an licks his lips. He's been searching for a quick mark, a young girl who won't put up much up of a fight. He intimidates them into keeping their mouths shut. He hadn't expected to see Kate here at the grocery store, least of all with Marnie. He'd been watching her for over a month.

His ex-wife, Darcie, knew Kate, which is how he'd met her. He'd fantasized about her for years. Now that he was divorced, he planned to make his fantasy a reality. Dan saw her at the diner all the time. He always tried to sit in her station. He'll ask her over to his house to have coffee. He knows she'll come. Kate is friendly. Once there, he'll overpower her. She'll cry rape and threaten to report him. He'll laugh at her. "Who do you think they're going to believe, a policeman or some slut waitress from Ruby's?" That will be the end of any discussion of reporting him. He'd done the same thing before with a couple of barmaids from Jack and Jill's.

Dan knows he isn't like most other men. Sex for him is all about conquest. He thinks about it all the time. He sometimes spends weeks following his potential victims, anticipating how and when he will take them. The women are objects, nothing more. If they even smile at him, he considers them his.

An older teen girl stumbles out with two bags of groceries, too heavy to carry, and heads down the street in the dark. Dan knows this one—perfect. He gave a talk on substance abuse at her high school a couple of years ago, and she sat in the front row. He coached her soccer team when she was twelve, too. Her name is Deena. He pulls his Datsun up next to her and rolls down the window. "Deena, get in, I'll give you a ride home." He remembers Deena's mother works at the truck stop, and he arrested her once for DUI.

"That's alright. I'm good, Officer Sowers." Dan is pleased that she remembers him.

"Get in," Dan says firmly, using his police voice. She shifts the bags in her arms and comes around, juggling them, and somehow opens the back door. She places the bags on the back seat, closes the door, opens the front passenger's door, and sits. "Fasten your seat belt," he says. Once she's buckled in, he pulls the car away from the curb and considers the consequences of what he's about to do to her. He takes the bottle of soda out of the cup holder by the driver's side. "Have some." He passes it to her. "You probably need it after your walk." Consequences mean little to Dan. He doesn't feel they apply to him. Ever since elementary school, he's done things; even when he's been caught, he's seldom gotten in trouble. From molesting younger neighborhood children and masturbating in front of his neighbor's window to burning his parents' house down, nothings ever slowed him down.

"I am kind of thirsty," Deena says, downing half the bottle. Dan smiles to himself. This should make things easier, not for her but for him. "You missed my street. My house is on Turner."

"I know. Don't you remember? I used to take you and some of the other girls home after soccer practice."

"Yes, but why didn't you turn?"

"It's a nice night. I thought I'd take you down by the lake."

"I promised my mom I'd go right home. I have to watch my little sister."

"Stop worrying. I promise I will."

Five minutes later, they arrive at the lake. Deena's eyes are glassy and her head rests against the window. She puts up little resistance. Dan takes her home afterwards like he promised, minus her underwear. He took them off her as a trophy before he woke her back up. He puts her out of the car and says, "Don't forget. Keep quiet about this. I've already arrested your mother once. You wouldn't want me to arrest her again, would you?" Deena shakes her head and runs to the porch. Dan has to carry the groceries to the door for her and leave them.

## Wayne

"I've worked out the details of your cover, Wayne. You'll be working for the Highway Department." Grimm's phone rings, and he glances at me. "Just a moment, I need to take this." He picks up the receiver and says, "Special Agent Grimm. How can I help you?"

Grimm's office is spacious and lined with bookcases. One wall has a mammoth window that looks over the Wilmette River. What a view. Someday I'd like to have an office like this. I take the thought back as soon as I think it. I'd have to read reports and someone would absolutely discover my secret. I scan the sky and remember how it was…

I struggled in all my courses. I failed most tests if they were anything but multiple-choice, because it would take me too long to read the questions and I couldn't finish in time. Homework was a nightmare. Reading what others did in fifteen minutes took me hours to complete. When I brought my grades home, my father would scream, "You aren't trying!" But I was.

Marnie was easy to talk to. I told her about my problem. She told me it's called "dyslexia," a word I had never heard before then. She said the school was required to help me if my parents asked for it. When I asked my mother, she replied, "Your father doesn't want you in a class with a bunch of retarded people."

"So what am I supposed to do?" I asked. "Hope nobody notices I can't read?"

"You can," my mother said.

"I can't." But my parents didn't want to hear it.

Marnie helped me. She got books from the library, read everything she could, taught me different tricks. She taught me to write the words in the air before saying them. It surprises me that she never followed her dream of becoming a teacher. She would've been superior to any I'd had. She had a way of breaking things down into manageable steps and explaining it clearly, even back then. *What if I have a child and they're born with this too?*

Grimm hangs up the phone. "That was your new supervisor, Herbert Bloom."

"Is it an actual job?" I lean in my chair, my heart racing. I'm getting a headache. I'll remember everything Grimm tells me about him. That is my superpower...my superior memory, but I can't work for them. Eventually, they'll find out I can't read.

"Of course not." Grimm shakes his head. "You know how this works. It's just a cover. Bloom knows the score. He'll order your business cards, make sure you have an office, and get you anything else you need."

I write down "H and a B" and his phone number. "When do I start?"

"Monday, if you can. How's your dad?"

"As good as he can be." I've never shared with any of my bosses that my father was abusive. All they knew was that he was in law enforcement, too, and that now he has dementia.

"Do you have an apartment yet?"

"I sign the lease tomorrow."

"Excellent. Leave your new address with HR." Grimm passes a piece of paper across the desk to me. "The latest arrest numbers in

California. What do you think?" I look at it. It's nothing but squiggles and meaningless lines to me. If I took it home and isolated each line with a ruler, I could decipher it after an hour or two.

"Umm, that's something." I nod my head. Should I tell him the truth? I put the stapled papers back down on his desk. Grimm squints as if suspicious, but he lets it go. I should've flipped through the paper and pretended to read it.

"Have you picked the people you want on your team?"

"Yes, I decided this morning. I'll work Josephine County myself. I want Turmoil, Alvarez, Dodge, and Pierce for the other areas."

"Are you sure, Wayne?"

"Why, what's wrong with them?"

"A woman for undercover?"

"She was top of her class at Quantico. She's qualified."

"Of course. It's just that she's not experienced."

"How's she going to gain experience? Being a woman is good in this case. They won't expect her to be an agent. Just like Hector, who's Hispanic, and Damon who's black."

"Well, if these are the people you want, I'll get them for you." Grimm picks up his phone.

Why shouldn't I have a team of people who regularly get discriminated against? It used to happen to me when people found out about my disability.

One by one, they file in. Rebecca Turmoil shows up first. She's five-four and has short red hair styled in a Dorothy Hamill shag. She smiles and takes a seat. Then it's Damon Dodge, over six-three once you count his afro; John Pierce, who has the appearance of a surfer; and Hector Alvarez, who looks identical to Erik Estrada. Could that be a problem? People thinking of *CHiPs* and assuming he's a cop? *Don't overthink it.*

Grimm nods to me, and I begin, "I'm starting up a task force, and I'd like all of you to be on it. Each of you has been chosen because you have a unique talent that sets you apart from others." I look at each of them in turn. "John, you're a whiz with computers. Rebecca, you come from an agricultural community. Hector, you're fluent in Spanish and you were born and raised in California. Damon, you're a martial arts expert and have a military background.

"I'm assigning each of you to a specific county. You will pick a town of your choosing and get assimilated. I only ask you to pick one as rural as you can. I want you to move there, rent an apartment or house, make friends, meet the locals, and watch what's going on. Go out to bars and restaurants, do your laundry at the local laundromat, and become part of the town. See who's moving in, buying property, setting up shop and growing marijuana. But be smart. There's a fine line between enticement and entrapment."

"What will you be doing?" Damon asks.

"The same thing as you, but under slightly different circumstances. I've moved back to the area where I was born and raised. No one there knows I work for the Bureau, so my cover's with the Highway Department under my real name." They nod their heads, and I look around at them one more time. "Any questions?"

Just as we're ready to wrap the meeting up, my secretary Janis bursts into the room. "Wayne, the Grants Pass police are on the phone," she says. "It's an emergency."

# 8
# bag of puppies

<u>Wayne</u>

During the entire journey from Portland to Grants Pass, my thoughts revolve around who killed my father. I can't come up with a single suspect. I pull in front of my father's house, now a designated crime scene, at three pm. Yellow tape is stretched across the lawn, and several police cars are parked along the curb, including Gary's. I tap on the passenger-side window and climb in. "How did it happen?" I ask him.

Gary's eyes are tired. "All I can tell you at this point is what the officer on the scene told me—two shots to the head, close range, .38 wadcutter ammo. They found a Ruger Security-Six at the scene, recently fired, and I know your dad owned one of those, so we're looking into whether it's his. It looks like maybe one perpetrator, but they aren't sure yet of even that."

"Can you get me the autopsy report?"

"Sorry, you'll need to go through proper channels with this one. The only reason you're not a suspect yourself is because your boss confirmed you were at the office."

"Anything missing?"

"I can't say for sure yet. The place is a mess."

"Yeah, I'm aware."

"No one moved the body, and the only blood splatter was on the wall in front of the chair. Seems like whoever shot your father surprised him and fired from behind. There were no signs of forced entry, either. Your father must have known them. And something else I should tell you. The detectives confiscated your pop's estate papers and took his will." He looks in his rearview mirror. "Huh, Marnie's here."

I look behind me and see her as well. "Alright, catch you later, Gary," I say, climbing out of his cruiser and walking back to Marnie's truck. I put one hand on the bottom of her window, and she gestures for me to get inside. Sitting down in the passenger seat, I ask, "How are you, Marnie?"

Her face is pale, and she looks exhausted. Her hair is pulled into a ponytail. "A better question, is, how are you, Wayne?"

"Fine, considering."

"Are you really fine?" Marnie's eyes lock with mine, and she removes her hand from the steering wheel, reaches out, and touches my face. "I used to say the same thing, but I said it to convince myself."

"I stopped loving my dad a long time ago."

"Abuse doesn't keep us from caring for someone. Why don't we drive somewhere quiet to talk? The Rogue River, maybe?"

I smile. "Like the old days? Remember how you loved to go swimming down at the boat launch wayside?"

"Yep. We had a lot of fun…until…" Then her smile and words fade. She starts the truck and peels away from the curb.

"Take it easy. One death today is enough," I say under my breath as the sun begins to disappears behind a cloud.

"So, what do you think happened? Is this going to be like what happened to my mom and everyone forgets about it?" Marnie cringes, shakes her head, and looks away. "I'm sorry, I didn't mean that."

"That's alright. As far as my father, whatever occurred, he might have deserved."

"You don't mean that," she says, glancing at me with worry painted on her face, and then back at the road.

About ten minutes later, we're parked under the Rogue River Bridge, watching the water glide by. She rolls her window down and then up again, over and over. "I'm sorry, I don't mean to keep doing this, but I'm nervous."

"It's okay, you don't have to explain it to me." I take her hand, and she leaves the window alone. It's rolled down, and the breeze blows throughout the truck, and the sound of the water and the thump of the tires going over above the bridge come in. "This was a good idea, Marnie. It's peaceful here."

"So will you move back to Portland now that your dad has passed away?"

I turn and get lost in her eyes. "He wasn't the only reason I came back. You're the other one. I let you leave before, because I lacked the understanding to make a wiser decision. I'm not going, at least not without a fight this time."

"I'm not worth sticking around for."

"Shush. You are." I bring Marnie closer and breathe her in. She smells like the diner; apples, smoke, bacon. "Don't send me away this time." I run my fingers through her hair.

"I'm sorry I did, but there was more to it." Marnie pulls away.

"Tell me."

"Now isn't a good time."

"Now is the perfect time. We can start over again. Please, Marnie." I can tell she wants to tell me something even though she hesitates, holding her hands in her lap and pulling her fingers before speaking.

"The men who murdered my mother…did more. I didn't tell the police the truth."

"Why not? What did they do?"

"The investigators asked me if the men touched me and I lied. I said no. I didn't tell the police because I was afraid. The men who killed my mother threatened to come back and kill me if I told anyone."

"What happened?"

"They…they raped me."

I take a deep breath, shocked to my core. "Oh, Marnie, I wish I'd known. I could have helped."

"What could you do? I was a mess and needed space. No one could help me back then."

"Is that why you broke things off?"

"That was part of it. You were also going to college, starting a new life, and I didn't want to hold you back."

"You weren't. You meant everything to me."

"I was stuck and I couldn't move on." Everything makes sense now. The Dear John letter I got. I should have known something was wrong and not let her go so easily. *What can I do to help Marnie now?*

The breeze blows in through the window and strands of her hair covers her face. She doesn't brush it away, preferring to hide herself away. "Do you suppose you could tell the police now?" I ask.

"It's too late. What could they do about it? Especially when they've done nothing about my mother's murder in all this time?"

"Did you see who they were?"

"No. They both wore ski masks. I only saw their eyes except for one of them. I saw his left hand when I tore his glove off."

"We should go back to your mother's house and search for evidence ourselves."

"I don't know if I can."

"I can, if you'll let me." I brush her lips with mine. Her lips are soft, even softer than the other day. I weave my hands through her hair and bring her towards me, sliding my tongue into her mouth. Marnie's tongue touches mine and they slide around together. She tastes delicious, like cinnamon. She trembles in my arms. I want more. "Can I touch you, Marnie?"

She nods and I move closer, gliding my hand under her jacket and then under her shirt. Her skin's like the petal on a rose, velvety. I run my fingers along the side of her torso, then up to her lace bra, sliding my fingers underneath and cupping her breast in my hand. I squeeze and caress her breast gently. She sighs. I move to her nipple, stroke it and it begins to harden. She sighs again. "Oh, Wayne." Her hand rests on my neck and we're kids again, necking in my car. I remember how much I wanted her, but I always stopped myself, because she was three years younger than me. I lower my mouth to hers and Marnie's mouth opens to my kiss.

*Caw! Caw!* A bird calls out, and another answers. We see them together through the windshield, flying, their wings overlapping, soaring through the sky. "I can't believe this is happening," she says. "It's been so long. I shouldn't be doing this. I don't want them to think I'm like my mother."

"Who's 'them,' and what's this got to do with your mother?" I bring my hand away from under her shirt and entwine my fingers with hers.

"The people who live in this town. If it wasn't for me, maybe the men wouldn't have had a key to get in."

"It's alright, Marnie. I'm here now. We're going to find the people who did this and bring them to justice. You won't have to live in fear of them anymore." I stroke her hair. "You won't have to protect yourself by yourself anymore."

Marnie pulls away from me. "I didn't I had my husband until he died and now, I have my sons to help me, and what can you do?"

"Of course, but I want to help you too. Please let me. I'll get the crime report for your mother's murder and study it. What happened to your mother wasn't her fault, and it wasn't yours either."

"How can you? You don't work for the police department. I can't even get an up to date copy of the report. I've tried. They treat me like I'm crazy."

Unfortunately, Bureau rules prevent me from telling her what I do. "I can probably get it through Gary. At least let me try. I also need you to try to remember as much as you can, even though it's painful." Marnie stares at me and nods. "What do you remember about that night?"

"I thought it was a nightmare at first. I'd been asleep. I heard a muffled cry. I thought my mother was the only other person in the house. Whiskers, my dog, started growling, and my bedroom door creaked open. A tall silhouette was in the doorway. Whiskers leaped towards the person, barking and growling." She smiles wanly, her eyes far off. "The lady at the pound said, 'No one likes black dogs.' I liked him fine.

"Then the man yelled, 'Motherfucker,' and hit Whiskers with something. He yelped. I jumped out of my bed and slammed the man with my fists, but he pushed me away and I landed on the floor hard on my rump. The man hit Whiskers over and over. When the moonlight hit it just right, I could see it was a knife. Even when Whiskers stopped moving, he continued to stab him. He said, 'I fixed your wagon, didn't I?' He then came over to me, put the knife to my throat, and told me to take off my pajamas. I guess I took too long, because he just tore my bottoms off himself. I clawed at him, which is when his glove came off. He slapped me and said he'd kill me if I tried fighting him again. That's when I saw the scar on his thumb.

"He flipped me on my stomach, and then I don't remember much after that. Then the second man came in. He stank of sweat and tobacco. He asked the first man what he wanted to do about me. I begged him to let me live. The second man wanted to kill me, but the first one reminded him that I hadn't seen their faces. The first man said, "Don't tell anyone what we did here, or else we'll come back and cut you down." She shivers. "Cut me down." She pauses a long time. "And then I heard their footsteps fade away. I don't know how long I waited…ten minutes, ten hours. Finally I ran to my neighbor's house and they called the police. You still think you can find the people who did this, Wayne?"

"I'll do everything I can." I hold Marnie and I've never felt closer to anyone. We listen to the cars above us as they pass over, *thump thump thump*. Then we see something thrown over the bridge. A white sack floats through the air like a plump ghost and lands in the water with a splash.

"What was that?" Marnie turns to me and grabs my shoulder.

"I'm not sure." We both get out of the vehicle and walk towards the water. The bag is near the shore.

"I'll fetch it," she says.

"No, I will." I wade in. The water gets deeper immediately, but thank goodness it's not cold. I'm up to my chest when I reach the bag and start dragging the bag back to shore. Things inside the bag move as I hand it off to Marnie. When she opens it, three puppies crawl out. She gathers them in her arms and they lick her face. We carry them to the truck and place them on the floor in the back seat. "It's a miracle, but I think they're fine," she says, examining them in detail. "It's not a dog-eat-dog world at all; it's a people-eat-people one. People are despicable."

How can I argue with her?

# 9

# default

<u>Marnie</u>

"Where have you been?" Kate asks as she sits on my porch's swinging chair. "I've been calling all afternoon."

"How long have you been waiting here?"

"Not long. Twenty minutes or so. I was just thinkin' of leaving. I hope you don't mind, I helped myself to some iced tea. Where have you been?"

"With Wayne. I stopped by to see him after I heard about his father."

"Why, what happened?"

"He was murdered."

Kate's eyes immediately get as big as saucers. "Oh my gosh! When?"

"I'm not sure when exactly. The police, literally just discovered the body. We drove to the Rogue River and talked."

"Talked, huh? Your lips are chapped."

"It's not like that." I see Cole looking out the door and I motion to him. "Cole, there are three puppies in the back of the truck. Could you put them in the kennel, check them out, and feed them?"

"Sure. Talk about good timing. I just got homes for two dogs from the sign I put up at the record shop. Where did they come from?"

"Someone tried to drown them. Threw them over the bridge in a sack."

Cole makes a face and shakes his head. "I'll take care of them, Mom."

"Wayne needs someone, and so do you," Kate continues, staring at me with sad eyes. "I like the idea of you two together. Don't blow him off, especially now."

"I'll try."

"Do more than try. For once, take a chance on love. You know it's the right thing here." She takes out an envelope bulging at the seams. "Anyway, the reason I came by is because Derek sold the next three pounds of your kind ganja." She hands the envelope over as she glances around.

"My kind ganja?" I say, frowning.

"Haven't you ever seen *The Harder They Come*? Some kingpin you are. Anyway, he told me he wants seven pounds next time."

"When does he want to meet?"

Kate screws up her face. "Er…nine o'clock tonight?"

I sigh. "Does he have a buyer?" Kate just shrugs and I continue, "He probably doesn't. Everything's a macho game with him."

"Marnie, do you have to be so skeptical of Derek? He's doing pretty well by you."

"Forget it. I can't believe you actually dated him."

"Why? He's good-looking and attentive in bed."

"He's pushy and narcissistic."

"No one's perfect." Kate smiles, sipping her iced tea.

I laugh at Kate's response. "I've got news. Cole told me the Bentleys' Lakehouse is empty this month. They're apparently over in Europe. And Cole's friend Melanie is their housekeeper and said she can give me the key." I wink.

"Oh, tell me you're not," closing her eyes and shaking her head.

"What's the harm? It's like they're getting a free housesitter."

"Marnie, breaking and entering is not housesitting."

"Do you want to join me or not?" I ask.

"I'll think about it." Kate stands up and heads towards her car. "I'll see you later."

Cole comes back from the kennel, and his friend Brent shows up. I make tacos for dinner, for my son's and their friend, but when I'm getting ready to leave, my sons start giving me the third degree. "Where are you going, Mom?" Cole asks.

"Kate's. She's having a Plasticware party."                    .

"Wasn't she just over here?"

"Yes, to invite me to the party."

"We don't need any of that crap," Cole sneers.

"Maybe not, but I still have to go and show support."

I'm preoccupied during the drive to the reservoir with thoughts about Wayne, the puppies, and everything else that's recently happened, which is probably why I don't notice the beams from the headlights further back following me. When I pull into the dirt parking area, no one's there. Did I get the time wrong? I stay in the car with the windows up and pop in an Eagles eight-track. In the distance I can see someone coming, but it's not Kate's Mitsubishi. Finally, it gets close enough for me to recognize the make and model, a Ford Fairmont. The car parks, Derek Live gets out of the passenger's side, and another man I don't recognize gets out from the driver's side. He looks like the Hulk minus the green skin tone.

Both of them stroll to my car and Derek rotates his index finger, signaling me to lower my window. I roll it halfway down. "Did you bring the product?" he asks.

"Do you have seven thousand dollars for me?"

Derek glances at the man, and they whisper back and forth. "Not all of it," Derek says.

"That's not how this works." I start my vehicle.

"Wait!" Derek calls out. "He's got enough for three pounds."

"Fine, slide the money through the window."

"Come on, Marnie, if you front him the pot he can–"

"No credit, that's the rule. You agreed."

The man's face turns ugly but he remains silent, removing a wad of bills and hands them to Derek. Derek counts it and then slides the wad of cash through the window. I reach under the seat, grab my tote, remove three one-pound bags, and hand them to him.

"I think we should—"

I cut Derek off. "Our business is concluded." I pull away, forcing them to step away from the car.

"Jack and Jill's, Saturday night at eight! We need to talk!" Derek screams. "And bring Kate!"

I was preoccupied with the deal going down, but not so preoccupied that I didn't notice another car parked three hundred feet down the road. As I get closer, I recognize the vehicle—Brent's clunker. Oh crap. Did the three of them follow me? There's no one in the car as I pass, but minutes later, the car whizzes by me going fast, and when I arrive home, Cole and Chester are waiting in the living room. Chester looks anxious, but Cole has a big smile on his face. "Jump back!" he exclaims. "My mom's a dope dealer!"

"It's not what it looks like."

"Really? Because it looked like you were selling three giant bags of weed."

I can't lie to my sons. "Yes. But I had to…we owe money for taxes on the farm, and your father, he—"

"We get it. Dad drove the farm into the ground."

"That's not true. He was a good man, a good farmer."

"Mom, you know that's not true," Chester says sternly. "He was lazy, bought too much equipment we didn't need, and planted things either too early or too late. If he'd listened to you more, we could've actually grown something."

"Where did you get the pot?" Cole asks.

"I grew it."

"Here?" they both ask in unison.

"Where else? Out in the back corn field. I did it to help with your father's pain."

Chester nods his head. "I wondered why you wouldn't let me help with the corn last summer."

"How much do you have?" Cole asks, his voice devoid of expression.

"Don't worry about that. I've got just a few more pounds to sell, and then we'll have enough to pay our back taxes."

"Finally, a cash crop we actually made money from," Chester says. "I'm proud of you, Mom."

"You shouldn't be. I'm breaking the law, and that's nothing to be proud of."

"Morality is an artificial structure created by society to control you. I don't buy into any of it," Cole says, his eyes burning brightly.

"Okay, Nietzsche, take it down a notch. Meanwhile, artificial morality or not, it's a school night, so off you go."

Groaning but obeying, the two walk off to their bedrooms, excitedly talking with each other about their mom, the dealer. I head for the long pine table where the four of us used to eat Sunday dinner as a family. I look through the mail, starting with the travel brochures. I sign up regularly for catalogs for round-the-world cruises and hotels in exotic locations I could never afford. It's silly when I've never been out of Grants Pass, and my only visits are to my rich neighbors' lake homes when they take vacations themselves. Still, I dream of taking a trip someday. Just me and Kate.

I see a notice from the bank marked "URGENT" and rip it open. What I read there flabbergasts me.

*You have now missed six loan payments. You are hereby informed that you have ninety (90) days to pay your balance in full or your assets will be seized.*
*Total amount with interest and penalties now due:*
*$501,326.77.*

My legs buckle underneath me and I slide into the chair. The room spins. The letter floats from my hand onto the table, the one that's been in Jack's family for over seventy years. I rest my forehead on my folded arms. I am now experiencing life at the speed of sixty What The Fucks per minute, and have no idea what to do next.

# 10
# doors open

<u>Wayne</u>

The police department finally let me enter my father's house last night. I decided to wait until daylight and return Sunday morning. I don't have a key and have to drive to the police department and pick one up. That's when the captain gives me a copy of Dad's will and informs me I've inherited everything.

My father's yard appears even worse than when I arrived in town. It may be late spring, but it looks more like winter. The sky is gray, and the rain is coming down in ribbons. Several pieces of yellow tape have blown free from the wire fence and twist in the wind. None of the neighbors are in their yards, contributing to the desolate scene.

I put the key in the lock, and the door opens easily. Every shade is drawn. The room is dark, crowded, and still full of junk and debris. The first thing I'm going to need is a dumpster. I'll have to go through all his things. I'd still like to know if my father had anything to do with my brother or my mother's deaths, even though talking with him made me think he didn't. I open the box of trash bags I brought with me and slip one out. I begin picking up and examining pieces of paper lying on the carpet, reading them and deciding what's worth keeping. An hour later I've done nothing but throw things away, but at least I've cleared an area by the couch.

I move on to the end tables where a stack of books is piled. My father didn't read much, but my mother enjoyed it. I eye them suspiciously and pick up her large black Bible that she read every day located in the middle of the bunch. She's been gone for a long time. Why is this out? I pick it up and thumb through it and find a white piece of paper folded in thirds. There's a message written in block letters:

*Tell him nothing.*
*Remember, I did you a favor. Be quiet or else!*

I try to imagine who could have written it and can't. What does it mean? Does it have anything to do with my mother? I keep the paper and put it back on the end table. I keep plowing through the random letters, mountains of newspapers, and piles of magazines until I've got twenty-five bags filled. I've used the whole box of trash bags, but there's still at least an entire box of bags' more to go. I'll have to stop for now and resume tomorrow. I'm surprised when I look at the clock and discover I've been here all day and it's now dinnertime.

I open the refrigerator and see there isn't much available, but scrounge together some cheese, bread and butter and make some toasted cheese sandwiches. After eating, I head to my old bedroom, which is now a den. The only things in there are my old desk, a desk chair, a photograph on the wall, and a dozen cardboard boxes of books and files.

I sort through the books but tire of it quickly and decide to go through the desk. When I tried to open it, I discovered I couldn't. I used to keep the key on the top ledge of the doorway, and thankfully, it's still there. Once I open it, I see that the bottom drawers are filled with green hanging files, that aren't labeled. I sit in the chair, prop the files in my lap, and start flipping through them. It becomes apparent they contain correspondence from various women. Some are love letters, others angry ones. They're all addressed to my father, and none of them are from my mother.

Some cards are still in envelopes with last names and addresses, and three of them cause my hands to shake. The return name is Melinda Monroe, Marnie's mother. I open and read them. Two of them are rather lovely, but the last one is threatening. Melinda says she's going to tell my father's boss he took advantage of her. I check the postmark date of the envelope. An accusation like Melinda's, if true, could've brought an end to my father's career in law enforcement, so I can't imagine what he would've done to retaliate.

I take the letters, bring them to the other room, and place them with the piece of paper I found. Is it possible? Was my father capable of doing something to Marnie's mother? If he did, would he have hurt Marnie, too? I pace up and down the hallway, pushing the thoughts away and attempt to calm down. I need to look for more evidence, not jump to conclusions. I tell myself to go rest and return in the morning. But then I realize I don't have to go; it's my house now. I can sleep here.

I find the linen closet, take some sheets out, walk into the master bedroom and flip on the light switch. It's better than the other rooms, not covered with papers and trash. I change the sheets on the bed, pop the old ones into the washer and call Marnie. I hope it's not too late. "Hello, it's Wayne," I say when she answers. "Did I wake you?"

"No. I was actually just thinking of you."

"You were?"

"Yeah, I've been out with Kate and I drank too much," Marnie says.

"How much?"

"A sugar-free Sprite and a Harvey Wallbanger. Kate talked me into that one."

"Lightweight!"

"I am."

"Guess where I am?"

"The motel?"

"Nope, I'm at my old house. I'm sleeping here. Do you think it's inappropriate, you know, so soon after my father died?"

"I can't say, but certainly creepy. I don't think I could do it."

"Why not?"

"The fact that your father was murdered there has something to do with it."

"You think I should wait a certain number of days?"

"Why? In case your ghost father still wants to sleep in the bed? Clang. Sorry, I dropped the phone and I didn't mean to say that."

"Don't apologize. That was funny."

"I'd have an alarm system installed. What if the people come back who killed him? Do you have a weapon, Wayne?"

"I've got my father's guns. He's got enough armory to open a gun shop."

"Good. Boobytrap the house, too. Put some pots and pans by your doors so they trip over them and make noise. I have a dog I can give you. You know I take in strays, right?"

"No, I hadn't heard."

"Now you know. A dog would be good to have. They bark the minute someone even parks in front of your house. They really are man's best friend."

"I'll think about it, Marnie. Are you sure you won't come over here?"

"Oh, you mean come over there with you, *now*? I thought you were talking about living in a house where someone was murdered. Do you want me to come over there, Wayne?"

"Yes, Marnie, I do. Would the boys be okay on their own?"

"They're spending the night with friends. Marnie says, "At least that's what they told me. As long as their story checks out, I'll be over in a half-hour." She laughs and hangs up.

I sink in my father's chair with the bear staring at me. I need to find someone who wants it or donate it. Should I have waited to invite Marnie over? The place is in a shambles. She's right. The house is creepy. Am I afraid of being alone? Don't be ridiculous. I'm an FBI agent. I can handle ghosts, even though Quantico did not provide training in dealing with paranormal entities. I search the house to brighten it up, and lo and behold, I find candles inside my father's nightstand drawer.

Thirty minutes later, Marnie arrives. "I'm sorry the house is such a mess," gesturing for her to come in. "I just started cleaning it up, and I'm afraid it'll take a while."

She stands outside and glances in. "Did you bring me over to help?" she asks.

I give her a knowing look. "No."

She gives me the same look back. "Good. Because I have other things in mind."

**MARNIE**

Wayne and I seem to understand each other without needing to say anything else. I reach out with my fingers and brush his chin, feeling his whiskers. He closes his eyes and groans. "Let's fool around," he says.

"I don't fool around."

"Of course you don't." He picks all five-foot-six of me up like I weigh nothing, carries me into the bedroom and sits me on his bed. His arms are solid muscle. The room is lit with candles and smells exotic, like the woods and roses. The idea that he did this for me is exciting. "Can I take your clothes off, Marnie?"

His words send a chill through me. "Please…"

He crouches down and slides my skirt off and then my panties, exposing my pussy. He places my clothing on the end of the bed.

"You're beautiful, Marnie." He gestures at my shirt and I nod my head, so he removes that too.

Now completely nude in front of him and feeling exposed, I've suddenly lost my voice and my nerve. I prop myself on my elbows and spit my words out. "Can I help you too?"

"That would please me, Marnie," Wayne says, hovering over me.

I sit up and undo the button on his chinos, pull down the zipper, then drop to my knees, remove his cock, hold it in my hand, and bring it to my mouth. It's long, thick, and throbs in my hand. I slide my tongue down the shaft several times and then around the head and stop. Wayne slides the head of his hard cock in my mouth a little at a time and then down my throat. I can hardly take it all in. My mouth is stretched as wide as it goes. "You're gorgeous, Marnie." I know he's going slow, for my sake, holding himself back, not rushing me, letting me set the pace. Wayne's getting turned on watching me, and that's turning me on. I look up at him and he touches my face. "Why don't you touch yourself, Marnie. Make yourself feel good, too." Jack never suggested things like that; he was never interested in trying new things that would increase my pleasure. It wasn't his fault. I take the blame for some of it. I didn't act interested.

I bring my hand down to my pussy, placing two fingers on my clit and move them down and then up again. It feels good, and I find myself responding to my own touch. Wayne begins moving into my mouth harder, and my pussy gets wetter. "I'm getting closer, Marnie; get ready." I nod and he thrusts faster. I close my eyes and keep sucking him, feeling the head as it enters and leaves my lips. My clit is swelling, and I know in another stroke or two I'll cum too, and I do. It's been a very long time since I've had an orgasm. An orgasm rushes through me, and it's all I can do not to lose my focus and clamp down on Wayne. Wayne yells, "Marnie, yes, oh, oh," and he spills his heat into my mouth. I swallow and keep swallowing.

When I'm done taking all he has, I stare up at him. "Was it good?" I ask.

"Of course. Couldn't you tell? It was outstanding. How about for you?"

"Wonderful." I blush.

Wayne pulls me to my feet, wraps himself around me, and kisses me. He puts his tongue in my mouth and kisses me lovingly. "That was truly lovely. I need some of you too. May I?" He slides his hands between my legs and finds my clit. My pussy is wet, and I groan when he touches me. He begins stroking me and I move towards him. "Lay down on the bed, Marnie." I do what he tells me. "It's your turn. Bend your legs and spread them wider." He dives down between my thighs, wraps his lips around my clit, and sucks softly, then brings his tongue up and down the lips up my pussy. He stops and says, "Oh, Marnie, I've had so many sleepless nights dreaming about you. Did you ever think about me?"

"Yes, Wayne, I did." I sit up straight and move away. "But I need to tell you something important. I don't know if this is the right time to tell you, but I don't feel right about being with you unless I'm honest about everything…about why I left school and broke up with you."

Wayne eyes grow concerned and he comes to a sitting position too. "Tell me."

"You know how the story back then was that I was in a sanatorium because of a nervous breakdown." I pause. "It wasn't true. I got pregnant."

Wayne's mouth opens in shock. "I never knew you dated anyone but me and we never had sex."

"I didn't date. It was from the rape."

"Oh, Marnie." He takes my hand, tears in his eyes.

"I went to this place in Maine. Saint Biddeford. A 'home for unwed mothers.'" I bitterly make air quotes with this last bit. "My foster-parents made me. That way, no one in Grants Pass would know about the baby. She was born right after Christmas. The snow was piled up twelve feet high. Everything was white and clean, and she was rosy and pink. She…she had big hands." I get a far-off look on my face. "I didn't even get to hold her. I knew if she stayed with me, I'd ruin her. I know I did the right thing, for her and for me. I'll tell her all this if she ever comes looking for me, but I pray she never does."

"I'm glad you told me. Does anyone else know? Your husband, your sons?"

"No, no one. But I wanted you to know."

Wayne smiles sadly. "It doesn't change how I feel about you. But if you don't want to continue right now, we can stop."

"No, I want to," I say eagerly, nodding. Wayne only hesitates a moment or two, then returns to his knees and dives back in. I can't hold still, so he puts an arm over me and holds me in place. He drives his tongue into my pussy, fucking me with it. I call out his name and thrust back. No one has ever sucked me like this. What am I talking about? Jack never did oral at all, unless it was me giving it to him. The truth is, he didn't like sex that much at all, at least with me. I know he had affairs but I never approached him about it, and I never blamed him. I married him when I was eighteen, almost three years after the rape. Perhaps he knew I didn't love him.

I let go of my thoughts and let what Wayne is doing to my body take over. He brings another hand up to my pussy, wetting it, and then places it underneath my rump. He brings his hand closer to my ass, gently putting one finger near my ass while thrusting his tongue into my pussy and then to my clit. "Oh, Wayne, you're driving me crazy," I sigh. I'm a woman possessed. I can't stay still even though he's pinning me down. There's no use fighting it; the last thrust of his tongue into my pussy does it. "Wayne!" I call out, somehow pulling his head and tongue towards my pussy. My orgasm seems to go on forever, and he doesn't stop, sucking and licking me and he tickles my ass with his finger until I stop moving.

"Was it enough?" he whispers.

"Yes. You're enough."

Wayne smiles. "You always make me believe I am. When I'm with you I don't have to pretend. About anything."

"Are you thinking of the dyslexia? You're not a kid, and it isn't the 1950s anymore. You can get help now without the stigma. We all have something that makes us different, Wayne."

"I feel safer if people don't know. I don't want them judging me."

"You're making a mistake. Real friends wouldn't judge you. And if they aren't real friends, get rid of them."

"Is that what you do? Get rid of them?"

"If they don't accept me the way I am, yes." I pull him into an embrace, and we spend the rest of the night in silent communion.

# 11
# vacation

<u>Marnie</u>

Jack and Jill's is crowded. Our town has little to do when we want to let our hair down besides fish, hunt, and drink. I don't approve of hunting which puts me at odds with most of my neighbors and I'm not much of a drinker either, which might explain why I don't fit in.

I grab a parking space, search under my seat, and find two of my hand-painted rocks before leaving the truck. One is painted like a lizard, and the other is painted like a frog on a lily pad. I place them near people's cars for them to find. I always hope someone who's meant to discover them does and will enjoy the gift, but most of them will likely heave them back into the woods or throw them onto the highway.

It takes me a minute to spot Derek and Kate once inside, but then I finally do. They've left a chair open between the two of them, but I refuse to sit next to Derek, so I move it to the other side of Kate before sitting down. "So, I'm here. What do you want?"

Derek takes a sip of his beer and stares at me before speaking. "Two things. To find out why you're such a space cadet, and to discuss the future." He's wearing a blue and white plaid cotton shirt and dark blue jeans. It kills me to admit it, but he's not a bad-looking man. Too bad he thinks he's such a Casanova. Some of the women stare at him and then back at Kate and me, trying to figure out which of us is with him.

"What makes you think we have a future?" I ask. "If anyone's the space cadet, it's you. You play fast and loose with things, and you constantly want to change the rules at a moment's notice. That's not how I operate. We agreed I wouldn't provide product without people paying first."

"Yeah, but–"

"No buts. I have five pounds left, and after you sell them it's over." I wave at the server to get her attention, who I recognize from high school, a former cheerleader named Becky. She dated Wayne before I did, and therefore never liked me. Her hair is dyed bright red now; she used to dye it blond. It looks good red.

She comes over, "What can I get for you, ma'am?" Okay, if Becky wants to pretend she doesn't know me from Adam, I'll play along.

"Sugar-free Sprite, please."

"Coming right up," Becky replies, balancing on one foot, spinning and leaving.

Derek huffs, "Can I get your attention?" Snapping his fingers in the air. "I have buyers for the other five." His eyes shift back and forth. "And it doesn't have to be the end. You could always grow more. A lot more. You have all that land, and apparently a green thumb for growing it." He grips the edges of the table.

I shake my head. "Even if I wanted to, I'm about to lose my farm. One of these days soon, the sheriff will be coming by to kick me out, and the last thing in the world I need is for them to find a bunch of pot plants and add to all my other troubles. It'd take a miracle to solve my money problem to allow me to grow more pot." I take a sip of Kate's Harvey Wallbanger. "Then again, I haven't shot you yet, so maybe miracles exist after all."

Derek's eyes widen and he jumps from his chair, like the Voyager shot into space. "Wait here a minute," he shouts.

"Where are you going?" I ask.

"God damn it, Marnie, will you just do what I say for once? I'll be right back." Derek sprints out of the door.

I turn to Kate. "Where's he going?"

"No idea. Maybe you scared him when you talked about shooting him." She gulps down her drink like she just ate the hottest chili ever and needs to put out the flames.

A few minutes later, Derek comes through the door with another man. He's blonde, taller than Derek, even more handsome, and wearing a white suit like something out of *Saturday Night Fever*. I nudge Kate. "Did they change Jack & Jill's into a disco and not tell us?" All the girls in the bar sit up straighter on their stools and stick out their chests. Kate and I glance at each other and burst out laughing.

Derek asks, "What's so funny?" when he gets closer to us.

"Nothing," Kate says.

Becky shows up with my soda and sits it down in front of me. "Sprite. Two dollars, please." She waits as I fumble around in my pockets.

Before I can find my money, Derek's guest reaches into his suit jacket and removes his wallet, pulls out a twenty, and hands it to Becky. "Keep the change and bring me a Stinger, darling," he says in a Spanish accent. He smiles, but it's not real; it's all teeth and doesn't reach his eyes. "You don't drink?" he asks, turning to me and sitting down.

"Occasionally. At home."

"It's best you keep it that way. A woman needs to keep her wits about her in environments such as this." What a chauvinist pig. Although he's right.

"This is Marnie, the woman I was telling you about," Derek says, gesturing at me. "Marnie, this is Rico, a friend. I've brought him here to talk about your situation."

"How do I know he's not a cop, Derek?" I take the napkin from underneath my soda, twist it around my finger, then untwist and shred it.

"Because I'm telling you he's not," Derek whispers bringing his palms together.

"This is ridiculous." I stand up to leave, bringing my napkin with me.

Rico stands up, too, and he's no longer smiling. "I can give you half a million dollars tomorrow, Marnie. All in advance. It doesn't serve anyone's interests for you to lose your growing fields."

"How do you know about that?"

"I know a lot about you. I can see that you know it's wise to be cautious in business matters, as well. Now sit." It sounds menacing at first and he seems to notice, because he then smiles and adds, "Please," gesturing to the chair. I lower myself without even thinking. "Don't be nervous," he says, gently taking the shredded napkin out of my hand.

"I'm not." I take the napkin back. "If all my money's going towards paying you back, I won't have any to live off of."

"I promise that the monthly payments will be much more agreeable than your current loan. You'll continue getting paid for each shipment as well. Not the thousand dollars per pound you're currently making, of course, but we can negotiate a new wholesale rate for the larger quantity. I'm thinking we start small for your first grow, one hundred and fifty plants this first time and you'll still earn a considerable sum. I'll provide a lot of other things too."

I bring one hand to my mouth and cover it, not wanting others to hear. "You've done this before?"

Rico leans back in his chair. He's relaxed but glancing around the place, keeping his eye on everyone. He nods. "We have a few farms in California already. Yours would be the first in Oregon. I find your product impressive. It smokes well. Smooth but powerful."

"I can't get away with growing that many plants in secret."

"I'm sure you can, but as I said, I have additional resources I can provide to assist with that. Camouflaged tarps for the plants. Selective bribes to local law enforcement. And I have an entire team of lawyers on my payroll in the unfortunate event of a raid. Everything comes with risk. With those two fields you have in the back of your property near the woods, one hundred and fifty plants or even more than that shouldn't be a problem."

"You've been by my farm?"

"Of course. As I've said, it's wise to be cautious in business matters. But I don't want to waste my time if you aren't interested. Are you?"

I give him a good, long look. "Let me think about it."

"Please, take until the end of the week. But be aware that you aren't the only farmer in the area I'm speaking to." He takes out another twenty and places it on the table. "For the rest of your evening. Señor Live. Señoritas." He nods at all of us in turn, then is gone as suddenly as he appeared.

THE BENTLEYS' LAKEHOUSE IS STUNNING. UNLIKE MOST OF THE OTHER vacation homes in the area, it isn't a log cabin, but instead modern and made mostly of glass. It's so close to the water that the dock comes right underneath the house.

I open the door using the key Melanie provided, sitting down on the oversized cream-colored leather couch and admiring the view. To be able to see the lake every day would please me to no end. Not that I don't enjoy looking at my fields, I do, but this is majestic. A few ducks fly across the blue skies into the clouds, then drift back and land on the lake's surface, pushing their heads under the water searching for fish.

*Brrinng, brrring,* the phone ringing, causes me to jump, and a recording says, "You have reached the Bentley's residence. Please leave a message, and we will get back to you, *beep.*" Then silence, and then someone speaks in a mocking tone. I recognize the voice, "I'm calling for the person breaking into—"

"Kate, I can't believe you—"

"I can't believe you," she says, "Breaking and entering."

"How did you get this number?"

"Cole gave it to me. How are you enjoying your vacation?"

"For the first couple minutes, it was relaxing, until some nitwit scared me with her phone call. Now I'm going to have to erase the message you left and change my underpants. I've never seen an answering machine before. This thing is a huge, black monstrosity. I hope I can figure it out."

"I'm sure you can. What are you going to do today?"

"Paint some rocks."

"Anything special?"

"I found one the other day, shaped like two fish swimming together. I decided to paint it and leave it in the garden for the Bentleys to find. I also have another one I want to make for Wayne. I'm seeing him tomorrow night.

"Did you decide about the other matter…growing for the suave, sexy, mysterious foreigner?"

"Only you would describe him this way and you aren't here to see my eye roll."

"How would you describe him?" Kate asks.

"As what he is—a scary drug lord."

"So answer the question. Are you going to do it?" Kate asks.

"I don't have a choice. I have to. If I don't, I'll lose the farm. When are you coming over?"

"In an hour. I'll bring some wine, watch you paint rocks and I'll paint my nails. We can sit in the sun on their deck and talk more about your new boyfriend."

"You mean Wayne?" I ask.

"No, Rico," Kate laughs and hangs up.

# 12
# sarcasm, wine & everything fine

**Wayne**

"Thanks for stopping after work to help me, Marnie. This has to be the last thing in the world you want to do. "

"Women love housework, haven't you heard? It's like our favorite thing to do."

"Hold on a minute, before we get started I've got to make one call. Hello, Will. I wanted to let you know as soon as possible that, um, I've decided to stay in my father's place instead. The number's 541-931-2400, in case you need to contact me. And of course you have my pager."

"Who's Will?" Marnie asks.

"My boss at the Highway Department. And I wanted to thank you, Marnie for the gift you left me, too."

"You found it?" Marnie's face lights up.

"It's extraordinary. The detail. You missed your calling. You're an artist. No one has ever made me anything so beautiful. It looks like a real lace-covered ceramic heart with violets on it. I had no idea you made it until I turned it over and saw your initials." Marnie blushes. She never could take compliments.

"I'm glad you like it," Marnie says. "Art, teaching, and flying were the three things I asked my guidance counselor about in high school, but she suggested secretarial school."

"What?"

"To be fair. She knew I didn't have money and you know…I had to take one year off and I wasn't ready for college."

"You were a good student. You could have done any of those things. Did you hear about NASA putting together its first group of female astronauts the other day?"

"I did. I wonder if they did it just to have someone on the spaceship to clean."

"Hysterical, Marnie."

"It's funny how much time we spend looking for intelligent life on other planets. We should spend more time looking on Earth first."

I belly-laugh. "So true."

She rolls her eyes playfully. "Where do you want me to begin helping you clean? It's a team effort, after all."

"How about my father's office, my old bedroom?" There are only a couple more boxes in there, and I'll be done with that room." I lead her there and point to a pile of books along the wall. "I found some empty boxes in the basement you can put things in. We can donate or toss it. If you find any papers that look important, set them aside."

"Who's that?" Marnie asks, pointing to a photograph on the wall. Her face suddenly turns pale, and she moves closer, staring at the picture transfixed. I stand behind her, looking over her shoulder. I recognize the man instantly.

"Dan Sowers, my father's partner from the police force." He's tall with piercing dark green eyes, and has a husky voice that used to scare me when I was a kid. Sowers was much younger than my father. He'd just started in the police force when he became his partner. My father brought him home several times for dinner. He and Sowers argued a lot. They also always made up. *They always had each other's back,* my father would say. Other members of the force referred to them as an old married couple. They certainly fought like one. In the photograph, Sowers has caught a fish and he's holding it up wearing hook-proof gloves.

"When was this photograph taken?" Marnie asks.

"I don't know."

She takes the photograph off the wall, looks at it, and then hangs it back up. "His eyes are green," she says softly. "The man who raped me had green eyes, too."

"How did you see them in a dark house at night?"

"The moon shone through my window."

"What else do you remember?"

"His voice was husky." The room spins. Was my father's partner, Sowers involved in Marnie's rape and the murder of her mother? Was my father? I feel dizzy and sit down on the bed. I don't even want to verbalize the thought to Marnie. I don't mention the letters I found from her mother to my father either.

She returns to sorting things. I didn't want to think my father was involved. It would ruin things between Marnie and me. I can't lose her again.

**Marnie**

Jack and Jill's is smoky and noisy as usual. Derek, Kate, and Rico are already there, waiting for me. Once I get settled, Rico asks, "What did you decide, Marnie?" I stare down at the square table where someone has gouged grooves. I visualize the letter from the bank lying unpaid on my pine trestle table at home. I imagine an auctioneer and people in our community bidding on all our things and my sons and me with nothing and nowhere to go. I think about what I will do with the dogs no one wants. I drum my fingers on the table. Rico puts his hand on mine and holds my fingers still. "Your decision, please."

"I'll do it."

"Very good." Rico removes his hand from mine, then pounds the table with his fist and flashes his fake smile again. "I'll take care of paying the loan. If anyone asks, tell them you've refinanced with Banco de la Republics in the country of Colombia. I'll meet you later to discuss the details. I look forward to doing business with you." He stands, pulls me from my seat and kisses my cheek. I pull away and he walks towards the door.

"You've done the right thing," Derek says, standing. "This is going to be good for you."

"If you're waiting for me to care what you think, we're going to be here a long, long, while." Derek doesn't say anything else, scurrying past me and catching up with Rico at the door.

"What do you think?" Kate asks, taking a sip of her drink.

"I think I'm fucked. I need a real drink. Where the hell is Becky?" When Becky returns, I order a vodka, cola, and Grenadine.

When Becky brings my drink she asks us, "So what's the skinny on those two guys you're with? They your dates?"

"Hell no," I say and shake my head as Kate laughs.

"They were good-looking. Especially the tall blonde one with the accent. He's choice and could rock my boat for sure," Becky says. "Plus, I need something to warm my feet at night."

"They're trouble," I say, taking a sip of my drink. "Ever thought of a dog?"

"Good to know," Becky winks. "I'm a bit of a nuisance myself." Kate holds her hand up and Becky high-fives her. I shake my head at both of them.

"Like I said, I've got a dog if you're interested."

**<u>Rico</u>**

"It couldn't have gone better," Rico says to Derek in his car outside. "But she's exactly as you described, bossy and stubborn. Where's the tape recorder?"

Derek pulls out a portable recorder from his jacket pocket and hands it over. "What are you going to do with it?"

"Hopefully nothing. But I might need it someday to encourage her compliance, or for my own protection."

"Blackmail?" Derek asks.

"I prefer not to call it that. Marnie is an improvement for me, a local with an actual brain. I can tell from her concerns and questions that she thinks deeply about what she's doing. And attractive, too, although she could stand some cleaning up. Have you had her?"

"You kidding? I'm lucky she hasn't shot me yet."

Rico laughs. "Yes, how do the American feminists put it? 'No means no.' So she knows how to handle a gun?"

"That's a big yes. Has dogs too and they aren't the small sweet, fluffy one's ladies tuck in their purses. These are nasty motherfucker's with fang's and torn off ears. Fighting dogs—Pitbull's."

"Really? And what is your friend Kate's role in all this?"

"She's Marnie's best friend."

"Humpf. Good to know. If I ever need to motivate Marnie, threatening Kate would be a possibility."

"You just met Marnie and you're already looking for ways to strong-arm her?"

"One must always be thinking ahead. Everybody cares about something or somebody." He gives Derek a once-over. "Except seemingly you. No roots, no girlfriend, no family, no house, not even a means of transportation. Other than not having a car—the classic profile of an undercover agent. Is that what you are, Derek?"

"Come on Rico, don't be ridiculous."

He raises one eyebrow. "Am I being ridiculous? I suppose. But for now, I must say my goodbyes." Derek takes the hint and exits the automobile. Rico leans back against the car seat and watches Derek walk back into the bar. Rico's father will be proud when he tells him they might have land in Oregon. He wonders if the man has figured out yet that he isn't his son. Probably not, or he would have already gotten rid of him somehow.

Rico must prepare the documents quickly before Marnie changes her mind. He can't afford to disappoint the man. Rico had learned to avoid doing so at all costs. One day in particular is burned in his mind. Rico had played an important polo game on a world-class thoroughbred his father had helped him buy. He hadn't played well. After the match was over, he cooled Viento down and put him away, but when he went back to the barn later to check on him, the horse was dead. His father had said, "You don't need a quality mount if you aren't going to play well." That his father was willing to destroy a million-dollar horse just to shame him had stuck with Rico. He never wanted to disappoint him in that way again.

Manuel starts the Cadillac and drives out of the lot and into the night. If his mother had stuck with keeping her husband and children happy instead of becoming involved with running the family business, perhaps she'd still be alive. Rico thinks yet again about who the man might be that she'd had an affair with. Who is his real father? He'd kept his mother's suicide note a secret from everyone in his family, even his brother.

## Marnie

Not even a week later, I find Rico in my driveway as I pull in after work, leaning against the hood of a Cadillac Coupe deVille, wearing shades and smoking a cigarette. Two more of his men are hanging about and scoping out my place. I pull my truck in next to his vehicle and climb out. "You shouldn't have come here. I have kids."

"The sooner they know about your new venture, the better," Rico says and takes another drag off his cigarette.

"Don't be insane. I have rules."

"So do I. One of them is that I don't take orders from others."

"How funny. That's one of my rules too." I spread my arms out wide. "This is my property, and no one tells me what to do on my land."

One of the other men with Rico walks closer to me, and Rico holds his hand up. "It's alright, Manuel. I'll handle this. Marnie, you fail to comprehend that 'your property' is now partially mine. That is what half a million dollars has purchased me. But perhaps you'll be more agreeable when I share what I've brought for you. Let's do so inside."

Cole's car isn't here, so he's still at work, thank goodness. Chester might be feeding the animals, or maybe he's with friends. I head towards the steps to the porch, and Rico follows me with his two men right behind. "Not them," I say, pointing back and forth between them.

"My bodyguards go with me everywhere."

"I think that's pretty funny, that you think you need a bodyguard when you're around me. Or are you worried you'll be attacked by a renegade cow?" I stop walking and, after a brief staring match, he directs his henchmen to wait by his car.

Once inside, we sit at my table. He pulls out a pager and slides it across to me. "My code will be 777. When you receive a page with that code, I expect you to contact me immediately."

I slide it back to him on the table. "I work at a diner. That's not feasible."

Rico slides it right back to me. It's like we're playing a game of air hockey. "My business is more important than your ninety-five-cents-per-hour job. I promise you, if I page you, it will only be in an emergency situation."

I slide the pager over to him again. "I'm not going to be at anyone's beck and call."

"If I leave with this pager, then I also leave with my half-million."

I stare at it for a long time, then reach over and slide it to my side of the table.

"Good. Next." He pulls out a sheaf of stapled papers and hands them to me. I start looking through them. "Your new loan. It is at an eight-percent interest rate, a bit smaller than your own bank's nine and a half. A three-thousand-dollar payment per month for the next 25 years."

"What if I don't make enough money to cover that?"

"I have not even the slightest hesitation that the Flower Queen will be successful enough."

"The *Flower Queen*?" I roll my eyes.

He smiles. "My brother's name for you, after he tried your product. They call the tops of the weed, bud, the flower. Now, sign." Rico hands me his pen, points to the signature line, and waits. He isn't smiling anymore.

I sit there, my hands covering my eyes for a moment, then quickly pick up the pen. I almost sign "Marnie Tillman," but then I remember my husband is dead. I think about the snakes that shed their skins, transform and change. I don't have to be Marnie Tillman anymore. As I sign "Marnie Monroe," I try to not think about the trouble I've just officially signed up for.

"Who is this?" Rico asks, pointing to my name on the paper with a strange look on his face.

"It's my maiden name. It's 1978. I want something that belongs to me and no one else." *Trouble here we come.*

"Alright. If that's what you wish. Next, we will discuss the growing of—" That's when I hear the sound of Cole's Mustang arriving, then a car door slamming. A minute later, his boots hit the steps of the porch, and then I see him walk in. He looks confused. "Who's this, Mom?" Cole asks and points at Rico.

Rico stands and smiles at him, offering his hand. "Rico Red. I'm leasing some land from your mother. I'll be growing corn on your property."

Cole stares at him and then at me. "Corn, huh?"

"Yes, corn," I say firmly. I give him a look that I hope conveys that he should drop the subject.

Cole shakes his head, gives out a "whatever," and stomps up the stairs to his bedroom.

Rico turns back to me. "So, as we were about to discuss. We've found it most effective in our other operations to create an indoor hydroponic room for when the plants are at seedling level, then only transfer them outside once they are mature. Do you have a place for such a thing?"

"I don't want to grow indoors. If I do, I'll need to use electricity. That costs money, plus it will attract the authorities. Suddenly I go from using a certain amount of electric power to using three times the amount."

"You don't know this for sure. What do you propose?"

I force the seeds between paper towels, once I do, I plant, transfer them outside in a protected space."

"This seems silly. This might have worked for forty or fifty, but you are growing three times as many and then how will you protect them when you first move them outside? You have something for that?"

"I still think it will work. I had something for hardening fifty plants outdoors, not for one hundred and fifty." I think about it a moment. "My sons and I will build something."

"I have men who can do that. Work on a list of additional supplies you'll need and I'll come back in two days."

"No," I reply. "I'll meet you somewhere neutral with the list, when I'm good and ready."

Rico smiles. "I find this place more suitable. I feel comfortable here. How does that American phrase go? 'Big sky country.'" He stands up. "In two days, then."

# 13
# puzzles

<u>Wayne</u>

It's a day of checking in with my task force over the phone. I start with Hector. "How's it going there in Trinity?"

"Great. I rented a place in Mad River. I might have a lead on a farm job. I figure it'll keep me abreast of what's happening. I've had one lead so far, something I heard at a Spanish bar here. There's a Colombian guy who has several farms in California growing bud. Where they're at, I'm not sure. Rumor has it that he's starting one in Oregon. Supposedly it's in Josephine County."

"Really? Interesting. Alright. We'll talk again next week."

Next, Rebecca. "Hi, Rebecca. How are things going in Humboldt County?"

"I've rented a small house in Fortuna and I got a bartending job. I'm overhearing a lot of chatter. I think there's a farm outside of town, but I haven't found it yet. People are very friendly here, but I can't ask too many questions yet. I do know that the farm is owned by a guy from Colombia named Red. Rumor has it that he owns several and opened a new one in Oregon."

"Interesting. Hector's heard the same exact thing. Fantastic start, but be careful. If you're going to do a drive-by, don't do it alone. Call me."

"Okay, boss. Chat next week."

I dial John Dodge's number next. "John, it's Wayne. How are things in Mendocino?"

"I'm living in the city of Ukiah. So far I've got nothing. The place is boring. I might move soon."

"Give it some time. You've only been there a couple of weeks."

"I'm going to hit a farmer's market Sunday. Perhaps I'll learn something there."

"That should work. We can talk next week. Visit diners where locals hang out and listen in to their conversations."

"Will do."

I save Damon Pierce for last. "Damon, how are you?"

"I've had a cold for a few days."

"I'm sorry. So where are you living?"

"Eagle Point, Oregon. It's one of the towns in Jackson County. I apologize; I was only able to get out and about for a few days before I got sick. One rumor I heard in town is that a Spanish guy is trying to rent some land to grow marijuana on."

"Description?"

"No idea. Tomorrow I'll hopefully feel well enough to go out and find out more."

"Sounds like a plan, Damon. I'll call back next week."

Hmm, interesting; two of the four have heard about something stirring here in Josephine County. I'll need to keep my eyes and ears open.

**Marnie**

"MOM, YOU'RE PLANTING THE SILVER QUEEN DENSER THAN USUAL," Chester says, looking over my charts for the coming growing season, that I'd placed on the table after clearing the Saturday breakfast dishes away, "And why so much room in between rows? That's not how Dad did it."

"Tell him, Mom," Cole says.

"Tell me what?" Cole asks.

I screw up my face. "Your father wasn't exactly an expert about farming."

"That's not what I meant." Cole lifts his eyebrows and holds up finger quotes as he says, "I mean about the 'corn deal' with the South American drug lord."

"You don't know what you're talking about," I say, staring Cole down.

"Don't I? Then tell me I'm wrong." He pauses and I say nothing, and Cole continues, "Yeah, that's what I thought. So when do the marijuana plants go in? Don't expect me to help without getting a cut of the profits."

"One more word, young man, and you're grounded."

Cole shakes his head. "That's rich, Mom. If you're going to do this, I should be a part of it. I could—"

WHOO! WHOO! WHOO! The alarm Rico had installed at the start of my driveway starts going off. He also spent thousands of dollars installing a six-foot-tall electrical fence around the entire property. Initially I didn't like the idea, but I have to admit I feel safer now. The only downside is that customers at the diner have started asking me questions. I told them it's to keep out the deer, but I know that's only going to satisfy people's curiosity for so long.

"Sounds like your drug partner's here," Cole says. "I don't know what use that alarm is going to do, by the way. Give you an extra thirty seconds to call your attorney?" Both of them leave the room and head upstairs, Chester with a worried look on his face while Cole just scowls. Moments later, footsteps cross the porch and then I hear several raps on the front door.

I walk over and let Rico in. "Good morning, Marnie," he says. "You have your corn now planted, yes?" He has a happy expression on his face. His smile has never been broader since I've known him. He's got a brown bag slung over his shoulder and he's wearing a white shirt, tan jacket, blue jeans and brown boots.

"Um, yes. My sons have spent the last several days planting."

"I've got the other seeds for you." He takes them out of a bag and passes me another package. "How are you going to germinate them?"

"I'll force them in paper towels for a few days and then plant them in seed cups. I've built the cold frame. It's behind the barn."

"Can I see it?"

"Sure, follow me."

I lead him out the door, down the porch steps, and past the pathway. Rico stops and points at all the snakeskin droppings. "A good sign where I'm from. Snakes keep rodents and insects away and it foretells increased fortune."

I lead him to the back of the barn. His bodyguard follows us. I've never talked to him directly, but he's even more muscular than Rico, with gray hair, mustache and beard. "Plenty of sun and protection from the wind back here," Rico says. "You've planned well, Marnie."

"I also thought I'd do a little experiment and try growing some down by our stream. The soil is richer down there."

"Whatever you like, as long as you stay on schedule. So far, I'm very pleased with what you've accomplished. Have you heard anything at work?"

"No, nothing new that concerns me. Maybe they suspect me and don't talk anymore while I wait on them."

"Do you believe that?"

"I'm not sure," I purse my lips and close my eyes briefly.

"You haven't done anything yet," Rico says. "You're most likely being paranoid. You haven't even started the seeds yet."

"You mean I can change my mind?" I swing my foot back and

forth nervously, kicking up dirt. Somehow, I manage not to kick any on Rico, but I wonder how he would have handled it if I did.

"Do you wish to?"

I've been afraid of one thing or another since I was a teenager, but for whatever reason I want to do this. I simply shake my head and say, "No."

He smiles, then suddenly takes me in his arms and kisses me. His lips are firm and soft at the same time. The sun is shining down on us. I don't want to like it, but I do. He smells like vanilla and musk. He swirls his tongue in my mouth. I know I shouldn't be doing this. I want to pull away, but I don't. I feel alive.

Eventually he stops kissing me, then takes my hand and leads me into the barn. "Show me around. What do you do in here?"

"Right now it's just for storage, but eventually this is where I'll dry the bud. It's perfect for that."

As soon as we enter, Rico closes the door, leaving his bodyguard outside. It's dark and quiet inside. I sit on a stack of hay, and he grabs both of my hands and stands between my legs. He runs his hand down my neck. "You like me, Marnie?"

"I don't know you that well."

"We will get to know each other." He lets go of one of my hands and slides his now empty hand under my shirt, towards my breast.

I know this is a mistake. "Not yet, please," and I stand up, forcing him to remove his hand.

Rico laughs, his eyes grow tired. "Maybe another time." He straightens my shirt, walks me to the barn door, and slides it open. We walk out into the light together, where Manuel is waiting. The sun shines down brightly, blinding me after being in the dark. "Marnie is an unusual name. Where does it come from?" Rico asks.

"My mother liked movies a lot. She was a fan of Alfred Hitchcock."

"Yes, I remember the one with the birds."

"Yes. He made another called *Marnie*, and my mother named me after it. It means 'from the sea.' Something sparkling, something shiny."

He smiles. "Yes, you *are* shiny sometimes. I will have to see the film now and see if you are like the movie. Your mother lives nearby?"

"No, she died."

"I'm sorry."

Rico walks me to where his car's parked, and Manuel follows. "Marnie. Keep me informed on how things go with the germination." He opens the car door and climbs in. I go up on the porch and wait for them to leave, wondering once again what exactly I've gotten myself into.

## Rico

"You like this woman, Rico?" Manuel asks as they pull away from her house.

He waves his hands in the air, unsure of how to word his response. "I find her interesting and I want to keep her happy. But she isn't easy to figure out. She kisses me back one moment, and the next she freezes in my arms."

Manuel grunts. "Her husband recently died. Perhaps she needs to get over him first."

"She'll be easier to control if she sleeps with me. It's how I do it with all the other women."

"*Si*, but it may cause problems. She has two sons. They may take offense. The one boy dressed in black makes bad faces at me."

"Yes, Cole. He does so at me too. You're observant, Manuel. If he becomes a problem, we'll have to remove him."

"The mother lion will protect her cubs, Rico. I don't think that's a good idea."

"It will have to be done with care, and only if there is no other way. But as you know, nothing must stop production once it begins."

## WAYNE

I'm at the grocery store and the cashier recognizes me. "Wayne, is that you? I heard you were back in town!"

"Yeah, Susan, hi. How have you been?"

But before we can get fully into a conversation, the bagger drops one of the bags he was loading up for the customers in front of me, a group of teen boys. It's clear that the bagger is mentally challenged, and can't be a day over sixteen. "Fucking retard," one of the teens says to the other, pointing and laughing.

"Hey," I say sharply to him. "Pay for your groceries, take your things, and leave."

"Are you going to make me, old man?"

I get up in his face, using the intimidation tactics we learned at Quantico. "Is this really the hill you want to fall on, kid?" I start taking off my jacket. "'Cause that's perfectly fine with me." The boy shoots me a nasty look, but he pays the cashier, snatches the bag, and stomps away without another word.

"Thank you," the cashier says. "Bobby here's a good kid. He doesn't deserve that kind of treatment."

"No one does." I pay for my groceries and head to my car. As I drive home, I replay the scene from the store. I could've been less confrontational, after all it was just a  teenager acting out. I tend to overreact when anyone picks on those with disabilities. Probably, because I remember when I could have been someone who'd been picked on if anyone had known. I also never spoke up when my friends had picked on others. I should have.

When I arrive home, Marnie waits for me, sitting on my front step. I fix her dinner and sit on the couch to listen to music. I do my old move on her: pretend to yawn, stretch out my arms, and wrap one around her shoulder. Marnie laughs.

"Good one, Wayne. Like I haven't seen that one before." She puts one hand on my thigh and squeezes. Marnie turns to face me. Her eyes are bright and seem to dance with light. She rises and bunches her skirt up, lowers and faces me and straddles my legs. She pulls her T-shirt up and 'surprise' she's not wearing a bra. Her breasts are white, and her nipples are the color of bubble gum. Marnie brings her nipple to my mouth, and my only thought is that I must have it. I swirl it in my mouth with my tongue and then suckle it. Her sighs start softly, then grow louder as I suck. She begins rubbing herself against my thigh, and I enjoy the friction of her panties against my leg. I bring my hand to her. I like that her underwear's damp. I move to her other breast and keep stroking her panties, and they grow wetter. She groans, "Wayne, please." I stop sucking her breasts. Her breathing becomes heavier. I rub her clit through her panties in a circular motion. I build up more momentum until she's bouncing on my leg. She's holding onto my shoulders, calling out my name, "Wayne, please," until she's rocking, her body shaking. Then she suddenly stops, her body collapsing over me.

"I'm sorry, I have to go."

"Go? There was no way I was going to stop unless an army of armed intruders broke into the house." I smile up at her. "Did you cum?"

Marnie giggles. "Not quite, but how about you? I can stay a little longer and help you out," and she runs her finger down my chest.

"Not if you have to leave, there's always next time. Are you sure you need to go?" I try to talk her into staying the night.

"I wish I could, but I can't," and she slowly gets dressed. "I can't leave two teenage boys by themselves. I'm sure you can understand, I just wanted to see you before I had to go home."

"They're sixteen and seem very responsible."

She scoffs. "You remember the stuff we used to do when we were sixteen?" Marnie says.

"Yeah, good point. But please be careful driving home. Those country roads are dark."

"I'm used to them. Been doing it all my life."

I bring her close and kiss her goodbye. She doesn't pull away this time. Afterwards I walk her to the front door, then to her truck and watch her take off. Just a few seconds later, though, a dark-colored Datsun parked across the street turns its lights on too, and suddenly takes off after her. That seems immediately suspicious, so I make a note of the license plate number and then run in and get my own keys, following the follower.

I pass the town square, then Ruby's, the laundromat, the bank, and then we're past the city limits. Whoever's driving is smart; they've left lots of space between themselves and Marnie's Chevrolet. I do the same with the Datsun. We pass dark farmhouses and pastures lit up by the moon. Suddenly out of nowhere, a lumbering form darts in front of me and I swerve to the left to avoid it, slamming on the brakes. Christ, a black bear. It gives me a curious look as it crosses in front of me and then lumbers off into the fields. I'm now stuck in a ditch and my car won't budge. Maybe the bear is a message that I need to exercise more caution.

Luckily, the ditch isn't deep and after a minute or two, I'm able to push my car into a free enough position to drive out. After another minute of driving, I come across the Datsun pulled over to the side of the road as well. I pull over and park, take the flashlight out of my glovebox, remove my Glock from my jacket, and proceed on foot. The Datsun is empty. I notice a black and gold decal in the back window that says "Support Your Local Police." Whoever the driver is, they're now on foot like me. I recognize the landscape. We've got to be no more than five hundred feet from Marnie's long driveway. What does the driver want with her? I think about cutting through her property, but I notice she's installed an electrified barbed wire fence. This must have cost some money. I stay on the grass that edges the driveway to make less noise, hoping whoever's here is preoccupied and doesn't realize they're being followed.

I'm not even halfway to the house when I hear dogs barking. I can't say how many, but four or five at least. The porch light comes on and one of her sons comes out and looks around. "Who's there?" he calls out, then goes back in. I crouch and watch but see nothing, so I head back to the cars; but once there, I realize the Datsun is gone. Somehow, he gets back to his car without me seeing him. He must have crossed over to the opposite side of the drive and stayed hidden in the trees. Now he's seen my car and knows I followed him. I return to my vehicle and drive back to my house, but the street is empty. The Datsun never returns.

I call work and leave a message on my secretary's machine keeping her aware of what I'm up to, "Janis. I need you to run a tag. Need the owner, address, and whether they have a record. Also, I have new contact information, in case Grimm hasn't told you." I relay all the new information, then ask her to contact me as soon as she has anything. I lock all the doors and set up the booby trap of pans, as Marnie suggested. I head to bed and put my gun by the nightstand. I have no trouble falling asleep.

I wake with a start, one of those times when you're unsure if you're still in a dream or if something's really happening. I hear *clang, gong, clank*, the pans from the booby trap crashing and slamming together. I reach for the gun and wrap my hand around it. Next, a silhouette of a figure appears in the doorway, but the man backs up and runs when he sees the gun. He slips on the metal pans and hits his head on the doorframe. He jumps up, and I'm on top of him. We wrestle over the gun, and it falls out of my hand. I must have practiced fighting with a gun a million times at Quantico. Now, when it happens, I turn into Freddie Fumble Fingers. *You've got to be kidding me?* My attacker manages to pull away, but I take hold of his leg, and he kicks at me, but I hold on. He kicks again, landing one on my shoulder, making me turn him loose. "Who are you?" I yell.

The man runs, crashing down the hall and because of all the

debris still in the living room ricochets against bags of trash, boxes, old furniture, and the pans I set up. Eventually, he reaches the front door, throws it open, falls down the stairs and sprints across the lawn, disappearing into the night. It happened so fast it's like he's a ghost who was never here. I question myself. Was it a dream? I go back into the house. The clock on the mantle says it's three a.m. My body trembles. I'm so wired, I can't even think about sleeping. Who was in my house? The same man who followed Marnie? How did he get in? I examine the locks on the door. None of them are broken or damaged in any way. It dawns on me that the man must've had a key, which means my father knew him. Is it the same person who killed him? I push a couple of pieces of furniture in front of the front door and do the same to the back.

Since I'm already up, I decide to go to the basement and search it. I haven't been down there since my brother was alive. I go down the rickety stairs, the ones I used to take with my brother when my parents fought. I flick the light on and a row of overhead shop lights blind me. My father kept a workroom here. He didn't have much patience with others, but he had endless patience for wood working. Too bad there was always something wrong with every piece; one leg too short, the finish too dark, a drawer that wouldn't open or close. We didn't care, because it kept him busy and away from us. Things were good until the furniture was finished, then he'd fly into a rage because it didn't turn out the way he wanted it to; he'd break whatever he'd built into hundreds of pieces.

Being here brings back memories, some I don't want to remember and still others, good ones I'd forgotten. There's a shelf with boxes of puzzles I used to get lost in. I would save my money and buy the most complicated puzzles I could; ones that had thousands of pieces and similar colors. They would require hours upon hours to complete. How had I forgotten something I loved so much? I take a few of the boxes down from the shelf and place them on the worktable to take upstairs. I remember my father saying, "You can't make a living from putting puzzles together." I laugh to myself; that's exactly what I now do. And just like those puzzles, I work on the corners and edges first, before the solution to the middle finally reveals itself.

I pass the large worktable and stop at my father's giant metal toolbox. I try to open it, but it's locked. I search for the key, but I don't know where he kept it. Where would my father hide something like that? I pull open the drawers of another work cabinet and find glue, sandpaper and pieces of scrap wood, but no key. I keep searching until I see a single nail and a small key hanging above the bathroom door. I grab it and try it, and the lock bounces open. The toolkit has twelve drawers, so I start with the top one, which turns out to be primarily screwdrivers and spare screws. I go to the next one, which has pliers of all different kinds and sizes. It keeps going this way until I get to the bottom drawer, which has no tools but is filled with odds and ends. I see a sealed manilla envelope, so I rip it open and spill it onto the worktable.

The first thing I see is a shiny black metal piece. It's one of those things you put outside that you hide a key in, but it's only the top piece. It's missing the bottom part. You can bury it in the ground or put it behind a flowerpot. Time stands still for a moment. I remember what Marnie said about her mother hiding the key to the front door for her so she wouldn't be locked out and the police saying they only found one-half of it. Is this the half they never found? If so, why does my father have it? Or am I jumping to conclusions, and is this nothing but a coincidence? I look at the rest of the contents but find nothing else significant. My head spins. I fold the still new-looking half into my hand, pick up the puzzles, and head up the steps with a sour taste in my mouth. Did my father have any role in the attack on Marnie and her mother? If so, my father was more of a monster than I ever thought possible.

I place the key cover with the cards and letters from Marnie's mother on the end table inside a folder. I head back into the bedroom and lay down again, but I'm still wired. I think about my brother, remembering the ping-pong table we used to have in the basement and how Mark and I used to play before my father got rid of it. Then he got rid of my mother and my brother. The ball bounces back and forth in my brain, like it did on the table, and I finally drift off to sleep.

When I wake up in the morning, it's past ten. I call a locksmith first thing and have him come out and change the locks on the doors, and add deadbolts too. I debate with myself whether to call the police about the attack last night, but ultimately decide not to; if I did, then I'd have to tell them about following the Datsun out to Marnie's farm, and receive a lecture I don't need. Best to let them concentrate on solving the murder of my father. Later, I come to realize that this turned out to be a wise decision, when I eventually find out who owned the vehicle that followed Marnie and I spotted outside her farm.

# 14
# collateral damage

<u>Dan</u>

**D**an agreed to Wallace's request for two reasons—Wallace's girlfriend, Melinda had a fifteen-year-old daughter, Marnie and Wallace was his partner. They had each other's back.

Dan's had a thing for younger females since high school. His father had sat down with him the first time he got in trouble. "You have to stay away from girls who aren't of the age of legal consent." After that Dan learned you had to hide your interest in girls who were under eighteen. He was lucky the first time; his father had made the problem go away.

He stalked Marnie for a couple of weeks. It was easy in his patrol car. He learned everything about her. She attended Walker High School, leaving school every day at 3:15 and walked home with a small group of friends, until she split off from them to get to her neighborhood, the poor one. She stayed late two days a week, Tuesdays and Thursdays, for chess club and art club. She had a few close friends but not a lot of acquaintances, like most teens do. Her clothes weren't fancy like the other girls, but she was much prettier than any of them, even though she didn't seem to try. She was taller than them too, but thinner.

Wallace wanted to keep his girlfriend, Melinda, quiet. Wallace was up for promotion and couldn't have anything stand in the way. Melinda worked at a bar; that's where Wallace met her. She dated him for a few months until she learned Wallace had lied and was married. Then she threatened to go to Wallace's captain and cause a stink. Wallace couldn't allow that to happen. If Melinda hadn't done that, Dan wouldn't have gotten involved. He called his friend Frank and visited Melinda to shut her up. The daughter, Marnie, is what some would call collateral damage. Dan called her fun.

It was an unusually hot April night when Dan and Frank came for them. Wallace told them about the metal box, by the side of the house, where the key was supposed to be hidden, but they couldn't find it. The house was completely dark. The temperature was almost eighty degrees, and the mother had left the living room window open. The screen was already torn, so Dan simply crawled in through the window and opened the door for Frank, then headed to Melinda's room. He found the key in the metal box on the dresser and put it in his pocket as a trophy. He gagged and tied Melinda to the bed for Frank. Frank did her and after Frank was done, Dan stabbed her to death.

Then Dan went into the girl's room. The dog, a Labrador-German Shepherd mutt, put up a fight, doing everything it could to protect the girl, but Dan stabbed it until it stopped moving. The girl tried to protect her dog, but couldn't do anything to stop Dan, of course.

After he was done with the dog, he went to Marnie. She was a good girl and cooperated with him. He said, "If you tell anyone what we did, we'll come back." Marnie must have believed him, because the rape was never mentioned in the eventual crime report. When Dan made detective and his commander had handed off a bunch of cold cases to him last month, he almost pissed himself when discovering that one of them was the same murder he'd been a part of committing.

Through the years he'd driven by Marnie's farm, thinking about how nice it'd be to visit her again; it had never been the right time before, but now with the husband dead and the sons getting older and not around as much, it was starting to feel like it might be the right time. He wanted a chance to tussle with her, to smell her again.

If Wallace had just kept his mouth shut, everything would've been fine; but after he had started losing his mind in old age, he had started talking about things he shouldn't have, and Dan had to shut him up. Now the son was back in town, too, and spending time with Marnie. Dan didn't like it. It would interfere with his plans.

Back in the present day, Dan exits the vehicle and walks the grass. It makes his sneakers wet. He hears a rustling sound and turns around, but sees nothing. Most likely raccoons. Then he hears another car. He turns and sees lights, so hides in the bushes. He stays hidden until he hears a car door slam, watching a figure passing him and sneaking up on Marnie's house. Dan quickly crosses to the other side of the drive and heads back to his own car. Thank God it's dark. Someone is parked in back of him. He checks the car. "Fuck," it's Wayne's Dodge Aspen. He climbs into his Datsun, keeping his car lights off as he puts the car in first gear and quietly gets the hell out of there.

If he can identify Wayne's vehicle, then Wayne will most likely be able to identify his. This isn't good. Dan's become sloppy. He should have hidden his car altogether. Dan thinks about adding Wayne to his hit list, but yet another murder would bring too much heat. Wallace is one thing; if he kills the son, it would bring even more questions. Dan pulls his Datsun into his garage, glancing at the boxes of pink pillows and cat paintings. After his wife left him, Dan removed most of her things, repainting the interior beige and brown and buying a comfortable leather couch.

Dan gets a beer out of the refrigerator, opens it, and picks up the phone to call his friend. "Frank. It's me. I need some help with a situation. Your daughter-in-law. Get your ass over here."

"You're such a sweet talker. Give me twenty."

Dan drinks his beer, thinking about the past and his options. When Frank finally arrives, he doesn't knock. He looks old and worn out. His hair has thinned and turned gray. Frank used to be muscular and now he's flabby. The years haven't been kind to him. "So, what's the problem, Dan?" Frank asks.

"I'm getting some pressure at the station to solve Melinda Monroes case and there's a lot of uproar over Wallace's passing." He hands Frank a beer.

Frank opens it, spilling foam, and chuckles, "I heard Wallace had some help with passing. What was it, two shots to the head? What does Wallace have to do with my daughter-in-law, Marnie?"

"Haven't you heard? Wallace's son Wayne is back in town and dating her again."

"It sure didn't take her long to replace my son."

"How much does she remember about that night? How much has she told Wayne? Did Wallace tell Wayne anything before he died? Is there anything hidden in the house? We need some answers, Frank. I think we need to put a scare into her to make sure she keeps her mouth shut. Maybe we need to ask Marnie some questions."

"She doesn't know who we are. We never took our masks off. You're worried about nothing. Better not to ask her questions, if you ask me." Frank slumps down in a chair, placing the beer on the armrest.

Dan thinks, *That better not leave a mark on the leather.* "Maybe she'll remember something small we didn't think about. Are you going to help me or not?"

"Yeah, sure, whatever you want, Dan. I don't like the bitch, but just so that we're clear, I'm not gonna help kill her. I have her sons, my grandsons, to worry about. I mean, look what happened to Marnie when we killed her mother. She went crazy and then ended up in foster care until she turned eighteen. I don't want that for my grandsons."

"Maybe they'd just marry an idiot farmer, like she did."

"Stop talking about my son like that. And don't forget the upside; we always knew what was happening with her because of me."

"What do you think your son would've thought if he knew you'd raped his wife?"

"Don't go there. Fate's a funny thing."

"That it is, Frank."

"God played an even bigger joke when my own father died and left the farm to them. It was a big 'fuck you' to me." He sighs. "So what's your idea, Dan?"

"A scare, nothing more."

"We gotta make sure her boys aren't there, especially Cole. The boy has weapons and can shoot. Marnie has weapons too, so we need to make sure to get her unawares. I've already lost a son. I don't want to lose my grandsons too," and a pained expression crosses Frank's face.

# 15
# deals & apologies



"**Y**ou're already behind?" Rico rolls his eyes. "Marnie, we had a deal."

"I had trouble germinating. Some of the seeds were inferior."

"My other growers aren't complaining. It could be the way you went about it. Paper towels, really?"

"That wasn't the problem. They probably knew to compensate by oversowing. I planted based on what I grew before. I'm sorry."

"Your apologies are a start, but it doesn't solve the problem." His blue eyes don't leave me. "I will bring you extra mature plants, but it will have to come out of your cut. And I cannot keep making up for your mistakes. I have partners too, and they will not be as patient as me." He opens his arms. "Now, come over here."

I change the subject. "Do you want to see the plants that are ready to go?"

"I do. Show me."

We go around to the back of the barn. I've lifted the roof of the cold frame. The plants have gotten larger and don't need to be protected from the weather anymore; it's getting to the point that they can't be contained within the structure.

"They're beautiful, Marnie. So healthy." Rico bends down and takes a closer look, touching them gently. "Such strong bases. How many are here?"

"One-hundred ten. I know I'm short. I've got another fifteen in the house I'm getting ready to bring out."

"Excellent. I will make up the rest with more mature plants. They will be twice the size as these."

"But they can't be taller than the corn."

"Don't worry, Marnie, they won't be. Your corn gets tall quickly. You said you also want to try growing down by your stream, yes? Take me there."

"It's a hike. You'll get mud on your fancy Italian leather loafers."

"Are you making fun of me?"

"No, but—"

"Go." Rico throws his hand out and drops in back of me. There is nothing left for me to do but to take him to the stream. The ground gets worse the closer we come to the spot where I want to sow the pot plants. The stream is a wide one, and it's muddy but the higher banks are an excellent spot to grow. "What do you think?"

"I think my shoes are ruined," Rico says as he stares down, pulling his feet out of the dark mud.

"I warned you."

"You did. Now let me give you a warning." Rico grabs my wrists, presses me against a tree and comes in for a kiss, but I dodge it.

"This isn't right," I say, escaping from his grasp. "We work together."

"I find love on the job makes things easier. Calms everyone down." He moves towards me again.

"So, all your growers are women you fuck?"

"Don't be silly, Marnie."

"Well, if you don't fuck your male growers, why should you fuck me?"

"I can see you're being irrational, so let's stop discussing the subject for now. How will you protect this spot from deer?"

"They never bothered the other pot plants when they were with the corn. If there's a problem, I'll install fencing."

We turn around and walk back. It's getting darker, and I'm growing uneasy being alone with Rico. I wonder about getting my knife out of my boot, and I'm starting to devise some scenarios to distract him so I can do it when I see Rico's face change. "A man is coming. Do you recognize him?"

Darn. It's Wayne. "He's…a friend of mine," I say.

Wayne waves at us, smiling. "The boys said you were down here. I was in the neighborhood and wanted to see if you'd like to catch some lunch." He glances at Rico. "Who's this?"

"Ah, yes. This is my friend Rico. Rico, this is my friend Wayne. We went to high school together." Both of them stare at each other suspiciously. "Let's head back to the house." Neither one of them talks, so I do all the talking. "How's the new job going, Wayne?"

"Fine."

"Wayne works for the state's Highway Department."

Wayne stares at Rico. "And what do you do, Rico?"

I interrupt. "Rico works in banking. A company his family owns."

"And how did you meet Marnie?" Wayne asks, looking at him sideways.

"I was having breakfast one morning at that delightful diner she works at. We began conversing about the financial predicament she finds herself in, and I thought I could perhaps help. After all, that is what I do." Wayne just nods his head.

As we approach the barn, I realize Wayne must've passed the cold frame and seen all the plants. Christ, how am I going to explain that? But when we get there, I notice that the roof has been partially lowered so that you can't see what's in it. Rico and I lock eyes and smile. My sons must've done it when they heard the perimeter alarm go off.

When we reach the front of the house, we see my sons sitting on the porch. They smirk at me. "I left my bag in the house," Rico says. "May I get it?"

"Will you fetch Mr. Red's bag?" I motion to Chester. A few moments later, he comes out with it. While Wayne's back is turned, I see Rico smile, shake Chester's hand. and slide some money into it. "Marnie, once again, what a lovely place," he says. "Wayne, a pleasure meeting you." He climbs into his car and drives away. The only blessing today is that he wasn't here with his bodyguard and driver, which would've brought even more questions.

"Where's Rico from, Marnie?" Wayne asks.

"Um, somewhere in South America, I think? Maybe Colombia."

He responds with the most obvious *harumph* I've ever seen a man give. "I've been thinking about what you said about having a dog for security. I think you might be right. I was hoping you might be able provide me one."

"Of course. What kind of dog do you want?"

"One that doesn't need much attention."

*People are all alike.* "I'll give you my best dog…if she likes you, that is. If she doesn't, I'm taking her back." I hate saying goodbye to Nova, but obviously it's for a good cause.

**WAYNE**

The dog follows me into the house and I close the door, bend down slowly, and take the leash off her. I have to admit, I'm frightened of her. She has one blue eye, one brown one, is missing an ear, and has a brown scar on her forehead that almost resembles an eyebrow. Marnie said someone used her for dog fighting, but she's surprisingly calm for me.

Marnie told me to keep my shades open, both because Nova likes looking outside, and because part of the point of a guard dog is to let everyone see the guard dog, which will scare away most intruders before any violence actually has to take place. She's right about that. The dog is pure muscle and looks like she could rip your leg off without even breaking a sweat. She spots the couch, takes a leap, barely makes it, and then spreads herself out on it like she owns it. I let her be. It's an old couch anyway, that's seen better days.

I check in with Janice, and it turns out she has information for me. "That tag you gave me belongs to a Daniel Sowers, from there in Grants Pass. No record besides a couple of speeding tickets. He's divorced. You might like to know he works for—"

"The police department," I interrupt.

"So you know him."

"In a way. Thank you, Janice. I have another license plate for you to check. A California Porsche. Anything you can tell me about the owner would be appreciated." I hang up.

Given what I already knew, I think it's likely Dan wrote that threatening letter I found in my dad's possessions. It said something about a favor. Did he shoot my father because he wouldn't grant him the favor? There's a connection here that I'm not yet seeing—Marnie's mother's letters, the metal key cover, and now Dan sneaking around in the middle of the night. I call Gary at home. "Any chance you can give me Melinda Monroe's file?" I ask.

"Sorry, but it's an active case, not a solved one. If I got caught, I'd lose my job."

"I understand. Who's the lead detective?"

"I believe you know him—your father's old partner, Dan Sowers."

"You're kidding." If Dan's in charge of the investigation for a crime he himself participated in, we're all screwed.

"Sower's a solid detective. Maybe talk to him and he'll voluntarily share."

"Perhaps." I leave it at that, hang up the phone, pack some tools, and head over to Marnie's old house. I'm relieved it's sunny, even if it's hot one.

# 16
# hard times

<u>Wayne</u>

Marnie said the neighborhood had fallen on hard times, and she hadn't exaggerated. I park my car out front because the driveway appears overgrown with weeds. There are also other debris blocking it, old bricks and pieces of wood. I immediately regret my decision to come by myself. Almost the entire street appears abandoned. The house is small, possibly a two-bedroom. I realize after parking my car it's not a house at all; it's a converted trailer. Originally it was white, but some thirty years later it's turned a dingy gray. The windows are shattered, so most likely the elements have infiltrated the interior of the home. I climb up the three concrete steps and grip the iron railing, that has now become loose. The frame of the storm door exists, but the glass is gone. I open it and try the wood door next. It's locked and doesn't budge. I circle around the back of the trailer. The door there no longer exists.

I enter the kitchen. Light from the open doorway allows me to make out the contents, a table and two chairs and an empty pantry. The floor is covered in old pizza boxes, newspapers, and booze bottles, most likely kids partying out here. I enter the living room next. More trash and cast-off furniture—an old torn couch with most of the stuffing gone, a chair and a large window with bent and twisted blinds hang down. My feet slide on the trash as I move towards the bedrooms where the murder and the rape took place.

The first bedroom is Melinda's. The bed frame is chipped and cracked, and a ghost of a chalk outline exists on the floor where the body was found. Or am I imagining it? The rest of the room is entirely empty except for the dried, faded blood splatter all over the wall and ceiling. I move on to Marnie's room, painted a pale faded pink. Her twin bed with no mattress and a small nightstand still stands. An broken lamp with shattered pieces of glass is spread about the floor. Books are strewn everywhere. I pick one of them up, *The Secret Garden*, and then another, *Are You There God? It's Me, Margaret*. I guess He wasn't, the night they were attacked. I place the books on the rickety nightstand. Anything valuable is probably long gone. It seems coming here had been a waste of time.

I hear banging noises and footsteps, and I draw my weapon. Then, there's the sound of a gun fired in quick succession. I shoot back and charge the two figures who flee down the hallway, one shorter than the other. They tear across the small living room, through the kitchen, and out the back door. They're both wearing ski masks. They cut through the backyard of another deserted property. I give chase but lose them as they cut through other people's yards. I end up lost, standing alone, surrounded by old junkers that people have left behind. A car engine sounds, and a compact grey car pulls down the street, but it's too far away from me to read the license plate or even make out the model. They were smart and knew to park far away from Marnie's house.

I return to her bedroom and search more carefully, sifting through the trash on the floor. I see it then, a single leather glove. Didn't Marnie say the man put it back on? Why wouldn't the detectives investigating the crime scene find this? I slide latex gloves over my fingers, pick up the glove, and carefully place it into an evidence bag. If it's the glove left by Marnie's attacker, it's over twenty-five years old; what are the chances of lifting a print after all this time? I search for the bullets that whizzed by my head. I find three in the wall, dig them out with my pen knife, and put them in another evidence bag. If I eventually find the weapon and the bullets match, I can arrest them for attempted murder.

## Marnie

I didn't want to call Rico, but I had to when I discovered it Thursday morning. After I told him, he insisted on coming for a visit that afternoon.

"I'm sorry, I didn't realize this would happen." A fourth of the pot plants I sowed by the steam are damaged.

Rico frowns and says, "You told me you would put up a fence if you noticed anything."

"I'm sorry. I wasn't feeling well and didn't come down here for a couple of days." Usually, I love it down here by the creek bank. It's peaceful—just me, the woods, and the running water—but now with what's happened and the way Rico's looking at me, it feels scary and ominous.

"This is the second time you've fucked up, Marnie. This is your job. If animals are getting into the plants, you must prepare for this."

"But that's the thing. It looks like someone damaged them on purpose. Look how the leaves have been pulled off completely. If it was an animal, the leaves would still be half-on from where they tried to nibble them."

"So someone is stealing from you. Is this what you're saying?"

"I'm not sure." My stomach flutters and my chest tightens.

"Which one is it? Should I question your boys?"

"No. They'd never touch them. It has to be outsiders, someone who's discovered them and wants to hurt me."

"And why would they want to do this, Marnie?"

"I'm…I'm not sure."

Rico sighs. "This of course is coming out of your cut, too. Let us understand each other. If anything else happens…" He suddenly grabs me by the throat and pushes me against a tree. I try to break away, but I can't. "Look at me," he continues. I lift my eyes to face him. "No more fucking around. My patience with this is over. Any more slip-ups and Manuel takes over, and he's not gentle like me. You understand?"

"Yes."

"Do you?" Rico squeezes my throat harder. I nod my head silently, and he finally lets go. "Go up to the house and fetch wire. Your sons too. Manuel and I will stay here."

I return fifteen minutes later with the boys. Cole says, "Fuck, Mom, it's growing here too?"

"Your mother is losing too many," Rico says. "It's causing a problem for her. If it keeps happening, I'm afraid I'll have no other choice but to do something about it."

"Are you threatening my mom, motherfucker?" Cole goes after Rico with his fists up, but Manuel quickly puts him on the ground. Chester comes at Manuel to help his brother but gets put down too.

I remove the knife from my boot and place myself between my sons and Manuel with my weapon raised. "Back up or you die right now."

Manuel's eyes open wide, and he steps back and looks at Rico. Rico smiles. "Are you sure you want to do this, Marnie?"

"You aren't giving me a choice. I told you before, my boys are off-limits."

"Your son struck first. Manuel has a right to defend himself. Put your weapon away, Marnie, unless you want me to take it away from you."

"I invite you to try." I hold the knife out in front of me. "Meanwhile, get off my farm."

Rico sighs. "You are very tiring, Marnie. I'll talk to you when you're more rational. Let's go, Manuel."

I grip the knife, my hand turning white, and watch them both walk the path toward my house, disappearing into the night. I then turn to the boys. "Are you guys alright?"

"We're fine, Mom." Cole climbs to his feet, pushing his chest and shoulders back out.

Chester nods. "You were awesome. What are you going to do about this asshole?"

"Work it out. But for now, help me install this fencing, please."

We spend the next hour and a half putting the fencing up. Whether it does anything to prevent the damage, I won't know until later. When we're done, Cole wraps his arm around my shoulder, his jaw tight. "We have your back, Mom. I'll shoot his balls off if he takes a step on our property again."

"You'll do nothing. I'm not going to war with an international drug king pin. Come on, it's been a long night. Let's head back to the house."

# 17

# psycho bitch

<u>**Dan**</u>

"I t seems dangerous to do this here," Frank says, rubbing the back of his neck as he sits in the passenger seat.

"Having second thoughts?" Dan asks.

"Yeah, Dan, it's my fucking daughter-in-law and grandsons, so I am having second thoughts."

"I've watched the house all week and it's the perfect time. Your grandsons go out every Friday evening."

"Maybe she's out too."

"Not tonight. I heard Marnie tell the other waitress at Ruby's that she's spending a quiet evening at home…at least that's what she thinks." Dan laughs. "Come on, help me camouflage the car." He points to a pile of tree branches beside where he's parked in the woods. If he'd done this the last time he'd come here, Wayne never would've seen his car.

They move up the driveway towards the house when suddenly the screen door opens, forcing them to duck behind a bush. They see Marnie come out and move down the stairs and the stone path, her flashlight hovering back and forth as she travels to the barn.

Frank makes a move to follow, but Dan holds him back. "Wait a minute. Let her get further ahead of us."

"Why don't we just go inside the house and wait for her there?" Frank whispers.

"Because she's armed to the teeth inside the house. We're better off catching her out here. Come on." They put on their ski masks and follow the bouncing flashlight as it appears and disappears between the trees. They follow keeping their distance and then speed up their steps, until Marnie hears them, and turns the flashlight in their direction. She screams and attempts to run, but Dan sprints and tackles her, making her land on her back.

"Is this your idea of punishment, Rico?" she cries, striking out with her hands. Her fingers just miss poking his eye, but her nails catch his arm. She reaches up again and pulls a piece of his hair sticking out from his mask. Next, she makes her hand into a fist and starts punching him in the throat. She tries to bite his hand but's he's wearing gloves. He's able to capture her hands and pin them to the ground. She tries to bring her legs up to knee him, but he moves down further and straddles her waist, preventing her from doing anything further with her legs. "Derek, is that you?" she asks in a panic. "Are you trying to get a bigger cut?" Frank slips a bandanna into her mouth and after that she can't say anything else.

"Listen up, Marnie," Dan purrs. "I warned you we'd come back someday, didn't I? You've been calling the police too much, stirring things up, asking about your mother's case. I need you to stop. I want you to stop talking to Wayne Farr, too."

She freezes in place.

"I fixed your wagon, remember? I let you live the last time. Do you understand?" It's like he flipped a switch. Marnie's eyes grow defiant and she gets one hand loose. She's quick, reaches downwards, and comes back with something. She drives it in his shin. It's sharp and burns. "Bitch!" Dan sees it glint in the moonlight when she pulls it out. Dan shouts, "She's got a knife." Marnie scoots up and away, and Frank backs away, too. Dan remembers the well-known self-defense tip he learned at the Police Academy

—charge a gun, run from a knife—and he follows that advice, but Marnie has already taken off. She must have found her flashlight, too, because suddenly, it's just the two of them—entirely in the dark.

Frank whispers, "What the fuck do we do now?"

"Get back to the car." They both start running, or at least as much as they can with Dan wounded. He can feel the blood dripping, but his adrenaline is pumping, too. They spot Marnie's barn and relief floods through them, because they now know they're just another minute or two away from their car. But still, once there, Dan holds them back from leaving.

"What the hell, Dan?" Frank asks him.

"She's gonna come barreling out of here any second and we don't want to run into her on the highway." Sure enough, a few seconds later they watch Marnie run out to her truck and pull out of her drive, hauling ass down the road towards town.

"How long do we wait?" Frank asks.

"Until she comes home and she's safely inside." Dan ties a bandana around his wound, creating a tourniquet to stem the bleeding.

"I've been telling you about that psycho bitch for years. Out of her freakin' gourd. Stole my truck while I was drinking at the bar. Who does that?"

"Shut up. We created her, didn't we?" She'd smelled so good when Dan lay on top of her, a combination of pine trees and something musky he couldn't identify.

"I need to get home," Frank whines. "I promised my son's girl-friend I'd have her car back by twelve, and now I'm gonna have to clean your blood out of it."

"Shut the fuck up. I don't want to hear about your problems. I've got my own."

They sit in the dark another hour when finally the headlights of Marnie's truck flash as she pulls in the drive slowly. They wait another twenty minutes before Dan finally says, "Alright, we can go." They get out of the car, clear the branches, and get back in.

Frank starts the engine. "What are you gonna do about your wound?" he asks.

"Stitch it up or use Super Glue. Luckily, it didn't hit anything vital."

"Who do you think Rico and Derek are?"

"I have no idea, but we need to find out. She's more dangerous than I anticipated."

"I've been tellin' you that, but you haven't been listening. She's been a thorn in my side since the day she married my son. Now that he's gone, there's no one to keep her in line. She's lost her fuckin' mind."

"Next time we don't come without a hypodermic," Dan says. "I have access to a few things in the evidence room that will slow her down."

"That would do it, Danny boy. I know she likes her green."

"Her what?"

"You know, weed, grass. She likes to smoke."

"Good to know." That was the smell he couldn't identify coming off of Marnie. Dan drives slowly and keeps the headlights off until they're far enough away from her farm. "Does she smoke a lot?"

"Not until my son got sick, then they both turned into potheads."

Dan got an idea and smiled. He could simply pull her over and use some pot he'll find as leverage. It's not like he hasn't done it before. All he'd have to do is follow her home one night.

**MARNIE**

"I'm sorry, Mrs. Tillman, but Cole continues to be a problem. Every year he's getting worse. He's a threatening presence." The principal of Grants Pass High School is giving them both a serious look, while Cole slouches in the chair by my side and smirks.

"Can you explain how? I mean besides the drawings on the notebooks the teachers don't like and that he gets into fights sometimes and—"

"He corrects the teachers when they're teaching. He hasn't turned in a single homework assignment this year. I simply don't believe Cole wants to be here," the principal continues.

"Cole, is he right?" I ask.

"Hell yeah he's right. The classes are stupid. I know everything they're trying to teach me and to be honest, sometimes the teachers are wrong, they don't know what they're doing."

"Could he just get his GED?" I ask. "Would the school help with that?"

"Certainly. If what he says is true, he could graduate tomorrow."

"Oh, Mom, c'mon!" Cole says eagerly.

"Yeah, but then what would you do?" I ask. "Just hang around the farm?"

The principal speaks up again. "He could go to Rogue Community College. It just opened a few years ago. There'd be a number of options available to him—night classes, classes only a few days a week." His tone softens. "Look, we want to help out here. It's just that we can't have him disrupting the rest of the students. But if this is the path you want to take, we can assist you."

I turn to Cole. "What do you think? Is this what you want?"

"Do they have an aeronautics program?" he asks the principal.

"Not them, but several four-year colleges in the area do. If you go to Rogue for two years, you could knock off all your basic requirements and then transfer. You'd be starting as a junior at eighteen. Understand, however, your ability to get into those schools would be contingent on maintaining a high GPA at community college, and assembling some good references. Have you ever taken a flying lesson?"

"No, but I've always wanted to."

"You might want to go down to the regional airport and see if the owner down there would let you work there part-time in exchange for some flying lessons. It'd be a good way to start. His name is Ted Gavin. He was a student here." He gives a sour little smile. "A real troublemaker, and you can tell him I said so. He'll consider it a compliment."

After getting the details about the next GED tests, I walk to the door with Cole and out into the hall. "You aren't mad, are you?" he asks me.

"Of course not. I just want what's best for you. But are you sure about this? You really want to leave all your friends two years early? Miss prom? Miss graduation?" He responds with the most epic eyeroll in the history of snotty teenagers, and I say, "Well, okay, then you have my support."

"I have some other news," Cole says. "Melanie said that the Bradleys found the rock you left in their garden when you stayed there."

"Oh no."

"No problem, she covered for you. Said you're a 'local artisan' who likes leaving your work in random places. Get this—Mrs. Bradley's friend owns a gallery in Portland. She wants to sell your rocks in her gallery. You interested in talking to her?"

I smile. "Of course I'm interested." My rocks in an art gallery. Unbelievable.

# 18

# trust

<u>Wayne</u>

"Hi, Wayne, it's Janice. I got the background info on that California Porsche. It's registered to a Colombian corporation, Banco de la Republica. The individual registered to drive the vehicle is Rico Rojas, I only have the business address of the company, no home address for Mr. Rojas. I'll have to look deeper. Should I?"

"Yes, Janice. I'd like to know more about him."

"I'll call you as soon as I find out anything more."

Why would a Colombian banker be interested in helping out Marnie and her little farm? Something isn't right about it. I hear a car door slam. Nova's one ear is up and she's wagging her tail a million miles an hour. It must be Marnie. Seconds later there's a knock on the door. "Hey, stranger, can't stay away?" I ask, opening the door.

"Something like that." Nova licks Marnie hand while she pats her head. "I had a rough night."

That's when I notice the abrasions and scratches on Marnie's arms and face. "What happened?"

"I was attacked at the farm when I was outside taking a walk, by the men who attacked my mother and me."

She gets me all caught up on the events, including their interest in me. When she's done, I take her in my arms. "It's going to be alright," and I pat her back.

"Is it? I'm tired of living like this. I've been worrying my entire adult life that they'll come back, and now they have."

"What time do you have to be at work?"

"I have the late shift today, 9:15. I wanted to stop by before work."

"Why don't you lay down for a bit and I'll wake you up when it's time to go."

"I'd rather do something else to get my mind off things and refresh myself." She grabs my shirt collar.

"Are you sure, Marnie?"

"Yes."

I take her hand and lead her down the hallway to the bedroom. I can't wait to taste her mouth again. "Oh my God, what did you do?" She spins around and looks at me. "It's beautiful, like out of a magazine. It's so tranquil."

"I don't want it too tranquil," I laugh, pushing her down on the bed," and it moves, making her body shake.

"Woah. She gives me an incredulous stare, and her mouth falls open. "Is this a water bed? I've always wanted to try one."

"Yes. I purchased it in Portland. I've heard they're great for pressure relief, spinal alignment and fun to have sex on. Now that I have someone to share it with, I thought, why not? Can I help you undress?" I drop by Marnie's side on my knees.

"Alright, um, I guess," but I read confusion on Marnie's face, and she scratches the base of her neck. "It's totally different in here."

"I've painted the walls, removed some old furniture and trash, and added the water bed, but other than that, the same. I don't want to rush you. Lay back and relax. We don't have to do anything, you can just try the bed and see if you like it." I start with

Marnie's sneakers, untying, removing them, peeling off her socks, and stop and watch her.

"No, I want to. Keep going." I move to her bell-bottom jeans, unsnapping the waist and unzipping them. Her eyes are wide.

"Lift your derriere." When she does, I remove her pants and set them on the chair in the corner. She's wearing pink lace panties. "Those are pretty. Did you wear them for me?"

"Um, kind of. I remember you used to like pink ones," and she blushes.

"I did, not that you let me see them too often. You were such a good girl." I laugh, then peel them off and smell them. "You smell so good, Marnie." She turns redder. I put them on the chair too. I come back, torn between wanting to remove her top and bra and wanting to dive between her legs. Diving between her legs wins out.

"Oh, Wayne!" she screams out, wriggling underneath me. I put one of my arms across her torso to hold her in place.

"Doesn't it feel good? Do you want me to stop?"

"It does feel good. I haven't had someone who knows what he's doing…forever."

"I'm sorry to hear that. But I'm not really." I wrap my tongue around her clit, toy with her until she whimpers. "What do you want, Marnie? Do you want to come?"

"God, yes. Please let me."

"I'm going to make you come again and again, or at least as many times as we have time for." Besides sucking her, I take my finger and slide it gently in and out of her pussy. Her body shudders.

"Wayne, please, give it to me, please."

"Harder? Softer? Tell me what you want."

"A little harder but a lot faster."

I returned my finger and gave it to her as she requested. After just a minute, I feel her pussy clutch my finger, not letting go. She screams out, "Wayne, oh, Wayne, yes, please fuck me, Wayne."

"Are you sure you want me to stop?"

"Yes, fuck me, Wayne."

I pull my finger out and stop sucking her clit. She's wet, but more women than I care to remember complained about the size of my cock, precisely the girth of it. I hope Marnie won't join the list. She sits up, and I remove her T-shirt and help her undo her bra. She's gorgeous. "Lay back on the bed and spread your legs." Marnie's smiling up at me. I whip off my shirt and drop it on the floor. My belt, with the buckle, hits next, and my pants and under-wear are the last to go. I slip the condom on and bring my cock towards her pussy, entering her slowly. She's wet from me sucking her, but very tight. "Am I too big? Am I hurting you?"

"No, it's fine. Just go slowly."

I put my hands under her ass and position her, watching her eyes. Even though she said it doesn't hurt, her eyes tell me some-thing else. I'm also having other trouble. Every time I move, the water bed moves Marnie, too, creating a lack of rhythm between us and causing me to lose my balance. I get back on my knees again, take my fingers and stroke her clit some more, making her writhe against my hand. "Oh, Wayne, please," she cries. I take my tongue and explore her pussy some more, giving her a long session, teasing her open. I take two of my fingers and, while licking her nub, push them in her pussy, as she clutches them. By this time, she's soaking, groaning, her bodies shaking, and she's close to coming. I add a third finger to her pussy, and she's stretched wide now. I stop moving my fingers completely and she begins pushing her body against them, using my fingers to fuck herself.

I pull my fingers out, go to my pants pocket, get some lube, and return. "This will help too." I spread some on my hands, my cock, and on her pussy before trying again. Again, I go slowly; this time, there's more give, and her body starts accommodating me. I move in and out slowly. We get a rhythm going, but this time the bed moves with us continuing to make squishy, squashy, sloshy noises, making us both smile. Marnie has her hands on my shoulders and her thighs wrapped around my waist. "How does it feel?" I ask.

"Great, Wayne. You can go deeper if you want." There's trust in Marnie's eyes like before, when we dated in high school, before everything happened.

"Really?" I thread my fingers through her hair and look into her eyes. The pain that had been there is now gone. I go at her, pushing in further, and this time her pussy pulls me in.

"Oh, Wayne, harder," she gasps, her breasts round and full heave against me and move with the bed. It's like we're floating on a raft on a river somewhere.

"Are you sure?" She nods and smiles. I drive into her with a pounding need until I finally explode, and her pussy squeezes around my cock. I can't hold myself back, even though I wanted to give her much more. I'm panting now, our bodies now fused together and we sink into the sheets, enclosed by the warmth of the water bed.

Afterwards, I pull out. "I'm sorry I didn't last longer, Marnie. Next time." I go the bathroom and get a warm washcloth and a towel before returning. I clean her gently and dry her.

"How was it?"

"It was great. Now I can say, I've had sex on a water bed, but I really need to go. Thank you, Wayne." She kisses me and I help her out of the bed. It's not the easiest mattress to get on and off of, or should I say in and out of?

I drive my tongue into her mouth and swirl my tongue with hers. "Thank *you*."

Marnie goes into the bathroom. When she comes out, she dresses herself and we go in the living room. I start to walk her to the door when the phone rings in the kitchen. "Hold on a sec," I say. "It might be work."

I'm only gone a couple of minutes, but when I come back, Marnie is standing there, her face white with eyes full of fire. "When were you going to tell me about this?" She's holding the black metal cover for hiding a key in one palm and the cards from her mother to my father in the other hand.

I pause and then sigh. "When I found out more. I was going to tell you, Marnie. I just found them myself the other day."

"You've known about this for *days*?" She throws them on the floor and runs out the door. Before I can stop her, she's in her truck and driving away.

# 19
# butterfly gift

<u>Marnie</u>

Rico's blue eyes seem darker tonight, and the smoke in the bar creates a thick barrier between us. We're sitting at a table at Jack and Jill's, with another man I don't know, at the only place I'm willing to meet. Manuel is nowhere in sight. I just want to get this done and over with. Things are bad enough this week; finding out that Wayne hasn't been truthful has made me question whether I want to have a relationship with him. If I can't trust him—

"I like the dress, Marnie, and your hair. Very pretty," Rico says. I wonder if I look less conspicuous because I'm as dressed up as they are. I didn't want the people in this town gossiping about me. What would they make of me sitting with two good-looking men?

"Every time you say something nice, something bad happens to me," I say. "I borrowed a dress from Kate; she styled my hair and did my makeup." The fact that it's crowded and late and the clientele has half a load on, hopefully, will make me less noticeable. Perhaps no one will even recognize me.

Rico gestures at the other man. "Like I said, you look lovely. This is my brother, Diego."

The other man takes my hand and kisses it, which makes me roll my eyes. "I'm glad you were willing to meet us," Diego says.

"Did I have a choice?"

"We all have choices, Marnie," Diego's eyes penetrate mine. He's clearly the older brother. He looks a little like Rico, the same nose and facial features, but he's at least ten years older and his eyes are warmer.

I bury my hands under the table in my lap, so they can't see my hands twitch. Betsy puts my ginger ale in front of me and places Diego and Rico's drinks in front of them, some sort of concoction I've never seen before. Diego hands her money and sends her away. I can tell by her reaction she has no idea who I am.

"Rico regrets that things got out of hand the last time you were together. He overreacted to the loss of the plants and took it out on you. He thought you may not have taken the loss seriously enough."

"Perhaps I didn't," I reply, throwing them a bone. "But after what happened to me the other night, I do now." I tell them about the attack, in the hopes that they'll help me.

Rico's and Diego's expressions change. Their faces turn white and the tendons on their necks tighten. I see a visible pulse. "Did you lose more plants?" Diego asks.

"No. I got attacked, not the plants."

"Who?" Rico asks, eyes narrowing.

"I don't know for sure, but I believe it's two men who've attacked me before, when I was a child."

"Are these the men we read about, who murdered your mother?"

"How do you know about that?" My hands become clammy and my heart races.

"It was public record at the time. We simply looked up the old newspaper reports."

"There's more to it. The men think I know more that I haven't reported to the police."

"Do you?" Diego studies me.

"No. Yes," I hold my breath for a second, then plow forward. "I was traumatized back then. They wore masks. It was dark. They killed my dog and my mother was killed in the next room. They also raped me. I've spent my whole life trying to forget what I heard and saw. I never told the police about the rape, because the attackers said if I did, they'd come back."

"So you think these men are destroying the plants to keep you quiet?"

"Possibly. Or they could've known where I was going and followed me."

"Did they say anything about the plants? Threaten to disclose you were growing them or anything like that?"

"No. They just said to keep my mouth shut and stop calling the police, or they'd come back and rape me again, and this time wouldn't let me live."

Rico and Diego give each other a long look, then Rico says, "In these situations, we find it best to immediately escalate, so that the situation can be resolved quickly. Go ahead and call the police. Make them come back. We will give you twenty-four-hour protection. When they come, our men will make them disappear, and you won't have to deal with them anymore." Rico says.

"Would you?" I'm tempted, but then he'd have something to hold over me forever. "That's alright, I've lived with them for this long."

"If they are disrupting our product, they have to go," Diego says.

"I don't know that for sure and what about the police? Do we really want them snooping around my farm, full of illegal pot plants? I don't want that."

Rico changes the subject. "Let's talk about you and your knife." He lowers his voice. "If a man did that, I would have killed him, no question."

"I had to protect my children. Surely you understand that. If you want to threaten me or even beat me, I'll put up with it, but don't ever touch my boys, and don't punish me in front of them. Because then it'll be *me* killing *you*," and I point my finger at Rico.

"That seems like a reasonable request," Diego says. "In the future, any correction Rico has to do, will be done in private."

"Thank you."

"Rico realizes all of this is new to you, and he will work hard to demonstrate more patience," Diego continues, looking over at his brother.

Rico remains quiet for a moment, then smiles. "So we will begin anew and put the past behind us, yes? Let's shake hands and be friends again." Rico reaches his hand out and I take it. What choice do I have?

"And the plants?" Diego asks. "How are they?"

"They're fine. No one's touched them since we built the fence."

"When do you think they will be ready to harvest?" Rico asks.

"Another month before I see buds, and then they have to get milky. I don't want to harvest too early."

"Alright, very good. If you change your mind about your other situation, let Rico know. We can't have our product at risk because you are, understand? You aren't alone." They both give me a weak smile.

"Yes, of course, thank you."

The two rise and walk to the door. I sit at the table at Jack and Jill's alone. I won't leave for another fifteen minutes until I'm sure they've cleared the parking lot. I take the rock out of my pocket, the one I've painted with the butterfly and leave it on the table for Becky. I wonder if she'll take it home, throw it in the trash, or just leave it behind.

### Rico

"What do you think, Rico?" Diego asks as he gets into the passenger seat of the car.

"I think she looked very beautiful tonight."

Diego laughs. "That goes without saying. I give our Flower Queen first place for most beautiful grower."

"I've come to realize one cannot treat women like one treats men. Women are different, and a woman with children even more so. I made a mistake with Marnie and handled the situation wrong, creating the problem." Rico puts on his seat belt.

"Yes, and this situation from her past, this is entirely too much. Imagine being raped and your mother murdered while so young, right in front of you. It's made her unstable. It would have been nice to know this before we became involved with her. What do you suggest we do about all this?" Diego asks.

"You mean the attacks on her and the plants?"

"Yes. Clearly we must do something to protect our asset and our investment," Diego says.

"Put a few men on the property to keep an eye on her and the plants, regardless of what she wants. If someone comes back, we take care of them," he says.

"As you wish. I'm also concerned about this other man you told me about, this old boyfriend of Marnie's. Is he really who he says he is? All of sudden he shows up in town after many years away. As you know, FBI agents often use the cover of working for other government agencies," my brother says.

"I agree. Let's have our people check this man Wayne Farr, out. Thank you for coming with me, Diego. She reacted well with you here. You have much more patience than I do."

"I think the key with her is to remain calm. Threats are not going to work with someone like Marnie. Remember, this is her first grow. She's learning. So what if she loses some plants the first time? It will simply teach her how to improve. She is the kind of person that will be hard on herself and will learn from her mistakes. You will gain nothing from punishing her."

"You're right, brother, as always. Who should we put down there to watch things?" Rico asks.

"Let's put Zarco by the road to see who comes and goes, and Fuz and Aaron down by the stream to watch the plants. Let's give them camping gear and have them stay round the clock for now."

"They aren't going to like that." Rico raises his eyebrows.

"It's not important what they like. They do what we pay them to do. If they complain, then we can treat *them* like men," Diego says. They both smile.

## Marnie

I'M OUTSIDE OF TOWN, HEADING HOME FROM JACK AND JILL'S, thankful that the meeting with Rico is over, when a dark car pulls up behind me and a blue light flicks on. Christ, an unmarked police car. Just my luck. I pull to the side of the road. Thank God I hadn't been drinking, and stopped smoking pot a few weeks ago once all the chaos started. I watch in my rearview mirror as a man walks from his car and comes up to my window. He's not dressed in a uniform, but is instead wearing a black leather jacket and leather gloves. I don't unlock the door and only roll it down far enough to hear him. I don't make eye contact.

"Registration, insurance and license, please," he says in a neutral tone. I reach for my wallet inside my jean jacket and hand him my license. I lean over to the glove compartment and get the folder that holds the registration and insurance card, remove them and hand them through the window. He motions to the glove compartment when he notices the gun. "You have a license for that?"

"Yes, but it's at home." That's when I actually get a good look at him. He looks like Dan Sowers, Wayne's father's old partner, the man in the photo in his house. I suddenly realize I've waited on him at Ruby's, too. "Pardon me, officer, no offense, but you're not wearing a uniform and your vehicle isn't marked. Could I see your badge and confirm you're a real officer?"

He goes in his jacket pocket and pulls out his shield and then his ID in a plastic sleeve. He holds them both up to my window Daniel Sowers, sure enough. "I'm a detective, not a beat cop," he says.

"Why are you pulling traffic duty? That seems strange."

"Get out of the truck, Mrs. Tillman."

"I don't think so." I look through the windshield. I'm way outside of town on a deserted stretch of road.

"You can either voluntarily comply, or I can smash your window, pull you out myself, and take you to the station for resisting arrest. Your choice."

I sit for a few seconds, then unlock the vehicle and slip down from the seat. He has me stand in front of the truck while he digs around. Something doesn't feel right. Minutes later he says, "What do we have here?" while pulling out a baggie of pot.

"What is…" I stammer. "Are you framing me?"

"That's a pretty serious accusation," Sowers says, grabbing my arm forcefully and dragging me back to his car. He pushes me into the passenger seat, then walks around and gets in on the driver's side. "Okay, so we have possession and an unlicensed gun. But we can solve this right now if you want." He unzips his pants and takes out his cock.

"I see how it is now." Trying to maintain my composure, "Sure, whatever you want. When I tickle and squeeze a guy's balls, it makes him cum harder and I can do a better job if you take your pants entirely off." I smile. "I bet you want that, right?"

Sowers grins. "I knew you'd figure out how to play nice." He pushes his pants to his ankles, struggling to get them over his shoes. "There. Now get to work," and he moves to pull my hair and force my head down. I take my ever-present bear deterrent from the sleeve of my jacket, where I'd moved it earlier when Sowers made me stand in front of the truck. I give Sowers a direct shot to his eyes. "AAAH!" he screams as I grab his pants and jump from the Datsun. "You bitch! I'll kill you!" Sowers falls out of his vehicle onto the ground and tries to swipe at me, but he's effectively blind at this point and can't find me.

"You try doing anything, you'll have to explain how I got your pants and wallet, you piece of shit!" I run back to my truck and throw his pants into the seat next to me. As I pull away, I see Sowers in my rearview mirror, still hunched over, rubbing his eyes, his flaccid little dick now waving in the wind.

# 20
# bury him deep

<u>Wayne</u>

Time for my weekly check-ins. Damon first. "Things are heating up down here," he says. "Can you come down and check them out? There's an out-of-towner who rented a major piece of property, and the whole thing is shady."

"Sure. I'll be there tomorrow morning."

I call Hector next, who informs me the first farmhand job was a dead end and that he's picked up another. "This one's the real deal," he says. "Five hundred plants in the ground, easy." He laughs. "I'm in charge of watering them."

"Do you have a name?"

"People just call him 'Red.'"

"What does he drive?"

"A big ol' Range Rover. And you know that rumor I told you about last time, about the farm in Josephine County? It's happened. I heard him talking about it to another man. It's in Grants Pass, believe it or not."

"Christ, I haven't heard."

"Maybe I should be the boss, boss!"

"Save the delusions of grandeur for later. Nice job, H."

I end the call and call Rebecca next. "How are things going in Fortuna?"

"Oh, I pretty much hate all mankind. Working in a bar is hell. I don't know how other women do it. But I'm hearing a lot of juicy stuff. There's a big new pot farm that's just started, owned by a guy in his fifties named Diego. I went last night and got some pictures."

"Great job. Keep it up."

I dial John Dodge next. "How are things in Ukiah?"

"Going to the farmer's market was a smart move. I met a guy there and he opened the door for me. I pretended I wanted to buy some pot, and next thing I know, I've got a job actually working on a pot farm."

"You've got to be kidding."

"I'm not. I started throwing around a bunch of big words like hydroponics and said I used to grow my own, and now they think I'm an expert. It's not a big operation, and the guy who runs it is all hush-hush. All I do is help him water the plants, lollipop, fertilize, stuff like that. He's really paranoid, so I know better than to ask questions. I know he's not running it by himself. I think when the bud is dry is when I'll meet the guys higher up."

"I'll call again next week at the same time," I say. "Nice work, Dodge."

It sounds like either Diego or Red are heading all these up. Most likely members of the same family. And where is the Grants Pass farm that everyone's mentioning? There's over fifty major farms in this area, easily double if you count the smaller ones. Perhaps Marnie can help me. She works in a diner, she knows all the farmers, and she waits on everyone. She can tip me off if she hears anything and then I remember Rico at her farm a week ago. Didn't' Rico say he was there to help her with a financial problem? Could Marnie be the grower? No way. She'd never do that. I stop myself from thinking anything negative about Marnie; I pack the evidence I found in Marnie's childhood home and mail it Federal Express to the Portland lab.

Early the next morning I drive to Eagle Point to meet Damon at a diner in town. He hands me a report before he even sits down. "I know it's kind of long, but there's quite a bit of information in there. It's all the dates I spotted Diego on the property."

"Description?"

"Six foot, average build. Grey-brown hair, mustache, beard. South American accent, I'm willing to bet from Colombia. I can't get near the place. There's fencing all around it, and even one of those fancy locks with a code instead of a key. Men all over the place. Maybe tonight I'll find a way to get closer. All the details are in the report."

Should I tell him? Marnie said I should tell people the truth. "Damon, I'm going to be straight with you. I'm dyslexic, so I'll read this report eventually, but it'll take me a while. Having you tell me what's in it right now would save me a lot of time."

Damon briefly gets a look of shock on his face, then immediately turns professional again. "Not a problem. There's ten to twenty men on the property at any given time. Sometimes another man joins him. He drives a red Porsche and he's tall and blonde. His license plate is in the report. Something's definitely going on there, but until I can get closer or we raid the place, we won't know. The big news is that they seem to be building a runway."

"Hmm, that *is* big news. That would allow them to get the drugs out quickly."

"Why do you think that?' I ask.

"Based on all the heavy equipment they're bringing into the place. They've got to be. We could take a ride down there tonight. One of us could create a diversion and the other could get inside, take some photos and check it out."

"That's not a bad idea, Damon, perhaps no diversion at all, just both of us sneak inside. Let's do it."

We wait until midnight before heading out. The farm is located in a wooded area, and like Damon said, surrounded by high fences. However, there isn't much activity when we arrive. Some sections of fence have no power, so we use wire cutters to cut them. The terrain is thick with brush. We didn't anticipate the sticker bushes or mosquitoes to be as bad as they are. Nevertheless, they provide ample protection for the three hundred-plus marijuana plants we discover.

Damon is taking pictures when a guard spots me. He's taller and larger and gets me down on the ground quickly. I've got to get up and away from him. I can't get to my gun, and even if I could, if I discharge it I'll announce our presence to all the others guards. I feel the ground for anything else I can use as a weapon, and my hand lands on something cone-shaped and textured—a pine cone. I don't see anything but my attacker's face. I bring the pinecone up with as much force as I can to his angry eye. It seems to take forever to hit my target, but I know it's only seconds before the man screams, clutches his face and stumbles away into midnight blue. I run the other way as Damon comes towards me, and we rush back towards the woods and the car. My body is shaking and we're both panting, out of breath as we climb into the car. Damon starts his vehicle, hauls ass away from the farm and heads towards his apartment so we can nurse our wounds. It takes us a few minutes to get ourselves under control before we talk.

"So what do you think?" Damon asks.

"You're definitely right, it's an active farm and the runway seems real enough. Hopefully they don't panic and close things down."

"Is that a real possibility?" Damon's face full of concern.

"There's always a chance of that happening, but in my experience, criminals have a lot of confidence or don't take the hint. Most likely they'll think it's someone trying to steal from them and just double-down on security. Do you think you got some good photos?"

"I know I did. Some of the runway and all the plants too."

"Good. Give me the film and I'll send it in. Great job, Damon."

"Yeah, and all it cost us was getting eaten alive by mosquitos," Damon laughs.

I'm exhausted when I get back to my house the following morning. My whole body is sore, and I've got bruises over my backside, mosquito bites everywhere, and dozens of cuts from the bushes. I tried calling Marnie several times to talk things out, but no one answered. I hope everything's okay with her and she's still not mad and avoiding my calls.

## Marnie

It's been two weeks since my meeting with Rico about the damaged plants and the road stop by Sowers. There's been no more damage to the plants by the stream, and thankfully, I've heard nothing from Sowers. That doesn't mean I feel comfortable going down to the stream; I don't, because I still believe it was a person, not an animal, that damaged them.

"Do you want me to go with you, Mom?" Cole asks as he pushes himself away from the dinner table.

"No, you two do the dishes. I'm sure I'll be just fine. Besides, I don't want to hold you up, since you both have plans. I'll take a weapon and bring a dog from the kennel." *If they knew I'd been attacked down there, they'd really freak.*

"Take Hercules. He'd lay down his life for you, plus he needs a walk anyway," Cole says.

"Be careful Mom," Chester adds, frowning and glancing at Cole. "It's dark down there."

"It's better now. Rico installed some lights."

"Let's hope a low-flying pilot can't see it," Cole says, squinting and then standing, picking up his plate and carrying it to the sink.

"I mentioned that to him too, and he said that the low voltage plus the tree canopy will block it."

"He would know, wouldn't he," Cole sneers.

I grab the flashlight and my Smith and Wesson, take an antihistamine and spray my nose with some nose spray. I let the screen door slam behind me, then sprint across the grass towards the kennel and remove Hercules from his run. He pounces all over me when I snap on a lead, and I sneeze once. Together we travel around the barn towards the woods, Hercules running alongside me gleefully. Ever since the attack, I no longer wander around the property at night without my gun. Uneasiness creeps over me yet again. I'm looking forward to harvesting these plants and finally being done with all this.

The hair on my arms and neck stand and Hercules lets out a low rumble. Is someone watching me? I spin around and skip my flashlight across the field and then toward the woods but see nothing. I keep walking, getting farther and farther from the house, until I reach the stream. It's only dimly lit, but even this light is better than none. Hercules lets out another growl.

A gruff voice calls out, "I've been waiting for you."

I recognize the voice and spin around, losing my balance and dropping my flashlight. I aim my gun in the direction of his voice. "Keep away from me." My eyes finally adjust without having the light and a silhouette comes into view. He appears to be alone, or else the other one is hiding somewhere. "Where's your partner?"

"I didn't bring him this time. I thought it would be nice if it was just the two of us this time."

"I have a dog," I say.

"Should I kill this one like I did your last one?"

"I have a gun this time."

"So do I. Looks like we have a stand-off," he chuckles.

*Pow. Pow. Pow.* Three shots ring out in the quiet. The masked man falls backward into the stream. Hercules howls. I stare at my gun. Did I somehow pull the trigger by accident? No, the safety's on. The bullets came from behind me. I spin around. Hercules is barking and pulling at the lead, trying to charge at the three men in back of me. "Don't fire. We work for Rico and Diego," one of the men says.

I drop my gun, mainly because Hercules is pulling so hard on the leash, I need both my hands to hold onto him. "Easy, Hercules," I say, picking up my flashlight and moving towards the stream to the masked man. He's lying motionless. I shine my light on him. Blood is flowing into the stream. Hercules is still pulling at his leash, attempting to sniff the downed man. The three others pull him out of the water. There's a wound in his stomach, a hole blown through the mask, and another in his shoulder. "I'd like to see who he is," I tell them. "Could you pull off his mask?"

One of the men crouches besides the body and pulls what's left of the mask away from his face. "Do you know him?" the man asks.

"Honestly, it's hard to tell. There's not much left of his face." It has to be him. His voice sounded the same. Why am I refusing to believe?

One of the men goes into dead man's pocket. "His name is Daniel Sowers, he's got an official ID card and a shield. He's cop.'"

"He's a police detective." I don't mention that he's also the same man who pulled me over and threatened to arrest me if I didn't give him a blowjob. I suddenly wretch and heave up the contents of my dinner.

"Fuck, we killed a cop," one of them says.

Another one says, "Aaron, page Rico and tell him to get down here fast. This is a problem." He turns to me, "Take a seat, *señorita*."

"I want to go back to my house."

"No, you stay right here." He scoops up my gun. "Is this the guy who bothered you the last time you were down here?"

"Yes."

"Weren't there two of them?"

"Yes."

"Fuz and Zarco, circle the perimeter and make sure no one else showed up to the party late."

I sit down and lean against the tree, and Hercules settles in my lap. What can I do but wait for Rico? I wrap my mind around the idea that Dan Sowers, the cop turned detective, was my rapist. How many times did I wait on him at the diner and never recognized him? But then I flash back. He wore shades and I remember he was usually either wearing gloves, had his hands in his lap and or under the table. So who's the other man? Will I ever learn who it is, now that Sowers is dead?

An hour later, Rico shows up. He whispers to his men and then comes over to me. "This is no good. We have to make him disappear."

"So do it."

Rico moves close to me. "No. I mean we have to bury him here, on your property."

"Why didn't you tell me about leaving men here?"

Rico furrows his brow and inhales deeply. "My brother and I worried that you wouldn't react well to the news."

"Well, you made the right bet there," I say, flummoxed. "So what about the second man? If he knows that Sowers came out here and then disappeared, he'll think I had something to do with it."

"So what? What can he do about it?"

"If he's a cop, plenty." My chest tightens, like I might have a heart attack. "He can get a search warrant, bring other police, search the property and find all this," pointing to the pot plants.

"Let's deal with the immediate problem and get rid of this one." Rico holds up a hypodermic needle. "Did you know the man had this with him? He was going to use it on you. My men saved your life. Isn't he your rapist too?"

"I'm almost positive he is, but I didn't examine his hand, he has a scar."

"You can do it now." We walk towards the body together. I shine the flashlight on the body but Sowers is wearing gloves. Rico crouches over the body and asks, "Which hand?"

"The left."

Rico pulls the glove off and I shine the light on his now exposed hand. "It's faded, but the scar's still there."

"You have your answer, then. Be happy he's gone and got what he deserved. Now, go up to the house and let us handle the rest."

Fuz returns and says, "There's nobody else out here. What do you want us to do with him?" He points to Sowers' body. I hear the sound of the running stream and an owl's hoot.

"Bury him deep somewhere." Rico turns to me. "You go back to the house, Marnie. Pretend nothing happened. Tell nobody anything, not even your sons. The less you know, the better."

I'm almost to the barn when I hear two shots ring out and realize my weapon is still down by the stream. Why are they firing more rounds? Then I remind myself that they're professional killers and know what they're doing. *What have I gotten myself into?*

I put Hercules in the kennel and considered returning to the stream to retrieve my gun, but I decided against it. I'm relieved when I enter the house and discover my sons are gone. I hear the alarm go off, telling me someone is coming up the driveway to my property. Who's visiting this late? I look out the window. Crap, it's Wayne. How will I explain Rico's car being here in the middle of the night? And what if Rico returns and finds Wayne here? Will he think Wayne knows something he shouldn't?

I go to the door and wait, trying to keep my hands from shaking.

## 21

# bad blood

<u>**Wayne**</u>

Why is Rico's Porsche here at eleven at night? I debate whether I should even go in. What will I discover? Then I see a black bear run across the drive and dive into the woods. My second sighting in as many days. Native Americans believe that's a sign that the person who sees it needs to calm himself and proceed slowly. It seems like good advice. I exit the car, climb the steps, and tap lightly on the door. The porch light spreads a welcoming glow of warmth across the porch.

Marnie answers immediately. I can tell something's wrong as soon as she opens the old, heavy oak door. She's biting her lip and rubbing one hand on her jeans nervously. "What's wrong?" I ask.

"What are you talking about? Everything's perfectly fine," Marnie says, standing in the doorway. Before the words are out of her mouth, I notice what she's wiping off her hands—blood. There's also blood splatter on her jeans. Or am I jumping to conclusions? Maybe she's doing a little late-night rock painting? My eyes travel inside the room, searching for Rico, but I don't find him.

I follow her into the house. She puts her lips together in a tight grimace and refuses to look at me. Her gaze ping-pongs all over the place and lands on a picture of her children that hangs on the wall over her fireplace.

I take hold of her shoulders and make her look at me. "I know something's happened, and you need to tell me about it, right now."

"I can't." Marnie lays her head on my chest.

"Why?" I feel my stomach tighten.

"Because if I do, it could be the end of both of us."

My mind races. "What are you talking about? I push her away so I can see her face.

"I can't..." She lowers her chin to her chest.

"You have to." I pull her to the couch and then onto my lap. "Nothing you tell me is going to change the way I feel about you. I love you and always will."

"Are you sure?"

"Yes, of course. You should know by now that I don't say things I don't mean."

"People do it all the time."

"Is that all I am to you, just some random 'person?'"

"No. You're very important to me. I just don't want to lose you. Something happened with Rico. I've done something."

"What's that?" *God, please don't say you've slept with him.*

"He and I are in business together." She pauses, refusing to make eye contact. "...Growing marijuana."

Oh my God. Marnie's farm is the large growing facility all my people are reporting. I just refused to see it. I rub my face with the palms of my hands. I respond, "There's no way you did this without him having something on you. Be straight with me. How did he manipulate you?"

"The bank called in my husband's loan. Rico refinanced it through another loan at his family's bank."

I shake my head. "What else?"

"What makes you think there's anything else?"

I stare at her. "Because right now you're shaking like a leaf.

Rico's not here, but his car is. What's happened?"

She moves closer and holds my shoulders. "One of the men who attacked me the other night came back tonight and attacked me again. Rico's men shot him. I'm sure he's the same one who raped me and killed my mother."

"Sowers' dead?"

Marnie gasps. "I never said his name!" She jumps off my lap. "How did you know it was him?"

"He was my father's partner. With all that stuff I discovered in my father's house, and the photograph of Sowers, it just stands to reason."

"Have you found anything yet that proves your father was involved?"

"No, only the things you've already seen. So what did Rico do with the body?"

"I don't know. He told me it was better for me not to know the details. It seems he's not the only one who's keeping information from me."

"I guess I deserve that. But look, playtime's over. We need to call the police. You've got a dead cop buried in a hole somewhere on your property, and you know how obsessed cops get when one of their own is killed and then there's the illegal marijuana plants."

"I can't. I'll lose my farm and end up in jail. This is all I have. I thought you loved me." Marnie brings a shaky hand to her forehead.

"I do, with all my heart. That's why I want you to do the right thing." I rub Marnie's back.

"Then stay out of this." Marnie stands up from the couch and crosses her arms over her chest.

"I don't know if I can. I have something to tell you too." I feel numb inside, knowing what I have to tell her and what I have to do.

"Now what?" Her shoulders curl forward and she tilts her head down.

"I don't work for the Highway Department." I feel lightheaded, knowing that the next words out of my mouth might end our relationship for good. "I work for the FBI, Marnie. I was sent here specifically to investigate men like Rico."

Her eyes are terrified. "You mean you're going to betray me?" She turns away, clutching her arms around her body. "What am I going to do?"

"I can't just close my eyes to this. It's going to be alright. You'll get a good attorney. You won't talk to anyone until he works out a deal. You'll turn state's evidence, whatever you have to do." I move towards her house phone and pick it up, wishing I could go back in time.

Suddenly, Marnie's front door flies open, and Rico, accompanied by three men, bursts in. Rico's holding a gun. "Put down that phone, Wayne. We need to talk. You two, sit." Rico's eyes are ice cold. "I know you don't work for the Highway Department, Wayne. In fact, you have absolutely no public record at all after you left this town to go to university. That can mean only one of two things: FBI or CIA." I keep my mouth shut and just stare at him. "I don't know if Marnie has told you what went down tonight, but if she has, let me add one more salient point that even she doesn't yet know. If this policeman's body is discovered, it will show bullets from several guns, including hers."

"You bastard," Marnie says, stepping forward and shaking her finger at Rico. "So that's what those two extra shots were that I heard."

Rico smiles, then looks at Wayne. "No doubt you are already formulating plans to have her testify against me as part of a deal. I'd advise against it. I've taped most of my meetings with her, and I don't think what you can hear her saying on them would bode well for her. If you're interested in joining our side, Wayne, you'd be paid handsomely. If not, we can pretend tonight never happened and just move forward. Take some time to think it over. Good night. I'll leave Marnie's gun on the table." Rico and his three men walk out of Marnie's door.

Marnie turns to me, panic in her eyes. "What should I do, Wayne?"

"Finish the grow, like Rico said. Meanwhile, I'll turn in my letter of resignation tomorrow."

"What? You can't!" Marnie takes hold of the sleeve of my shirt, her eyes pleading.

"I have to. I can't continue to be an agent, knowing what I now know. You understand, don't you?" My breath comes easier. I'm ready to let go for now.

"Yes. I understand I've ruined your career." Marnie's face is full of sorrow and tears fall from her eyes.

I smile and touch her cheek. "No you haven't. We'll figure out a way to get out of this. But until then, you'll fulfill your obligation to Rico, and I'll help you on the farm. But this isn't over." I take Marnie in my arms. "You understand? We're not giving up."

"I'm sorry I've dragged you into all this. I'll never forgive myself for what I've done to you."

"I'd do it all over again, Marnie. I'd sacrifice everything for you. I love you."

## Marnie

Wayne's pinned my stomach against the glass shower door as he lays on top of me. The warm water beats down on us. "I hope the boys are still asleep," my voice wavers.

"They've never gotten up before we have in the mornings, since I've been here," Wayne jokes, as he passes the soap over my shoulders, down my back, and then brings it between my legs, rubbing my clit in a circle. "I'm cleaning you," and a devilish smile crosses his face as he looks down at me.

"Why? You're just going to dirty me up again?" The scent of lemongrass and lemon permeates the shower.

"True, but you'll be in here so it makes things convenient, doesn't it?"

"You don't hear me complaining," I say.

"I didn't think so. Whoops, I dropped the soap," Wayne chuckles as his dark, wet hair falls onto his face.

"That wasn't an accident. You did that on purpose."

"That's right. So bend down and pick it up for me, please." Once I do, Wayne says. "Now stay there, that's the way." He comes from behind me while using one hand to rub my clit, and slowly brings his cock against my backside, teasing me. I feel the tip of his cock at the entrance of my pussy. At first, I couldn't manage him. He seems too enormous, but slowly, he slides in, stretching me. My body wants him and begins to adjust, slowly allowing him entry, a little bit at a time, until it pulls him in, his erection filling me. "Yes, that's the way to take me," Wayne says, letting go of my clit and taking my hips and driving his cock in further. "I have an idea," he says.

"You always do," I laugh.

"I believe it's the other way around," Wayne says.

"Okay, what's your idea?"

"How about we try the shower massager?" Wayne asks.

"Oh, that olde thing? I use it all the time."

"Do you then? We are definitely using it," Wayne reaches up, takes it off the wall, adjusts the nozzle, and turns it on before I can say another word. "Here we go then." He presses me closer to the shower wall, with his body on top of me so there's no means of escape, and brings the massager to my clit, which tickles at first but builds with intensity the longer it is there. He continues to slowly fuck me, but after a minute, Wayne flicks his finger on the wand and takes it to its most potent level while Wayne's deep, steady thrusts keep me on edge. I still can't believe Wayne's cock fits inside of me, yet my body desires him. "Squeeze my cock, Marnie," Wayne says. The words, the vibration from the water on my clit, and Wayne's hard fucking all come together; my pussy clutches his cock, and my muscles suddenly spasm around him. Like waves in an ocean that go on and on, I orgasm. Wayne shouts, "Yes, Marnie, go girl, go." Wayne's body jerks hard, and a fireball of heat pours into me. My pussy tightens even more around his cock, milking him of everything he has to give.

I lay underneath Wayne as the water from the shower beats down on us. I'm surprised that I'm able to enjoy sex. It had never happened before. "You were right about the shower massager. I'd never used it in this way," I say as Wayne's muscular body presses on me.

"Now you know how to use it properly," Wayne hands it to me, smiling.

**W**AYNE

I'm having breakfast with Marnie, Cole and Chester. Marnie told me the other night how much it boggles her mind that I've been able to get along with her sons so easily, but it's not actually that difficult. Like all teen boys, they simply want adults to treat them seriously and actually listen to what they're saying. That's easy for me to do, since I spent my teen years wanting the exact same thing. Chester's showing me some leaves from the plants by the stream they brought up this morning, which are displaying some kind of mysterious fungus. "Do you know what it is?" I ask.

Suddenly Marnie appears at the doorway. "I think it's Leaf Septoria," she says, coming over and joining us at the table. "Notice the black circles and the small amount of yellow going around it. I think it's developing down at the stream because it's too moist for the plants. Lesson learned, but we need to be careful not to spread it to the other ones up in the fields. We can carry it on our shoes and clothing."

"Are you going to tell Rico and Diego about this?"

"Absolutely Not. We harvest in just another couple of weeks, and next time we simply don't plant by the stream again."

"Is there going the be a next time?" Before Marnie can answer, the perimeter alarm goes off. I get up and look through the front windows, and see that it's Gary in his patrol car. I walk out, Nova follows me, and I shake his hand, "Morning, Gary."

"Good morning. Just the man I was looking for."

"How did you know to find me out here?"

"It's a small town, Wayne. News travels fast." He pauses. "I don't know if you've heard, but Dan Sowers' disappeared."

"Really? No, I hadn't heard." I hate lying to a friend and keep my poker face in place.

"I was wondering if you remember when the last time was that you saw or spoke to him. I remember you saying you were going to talk to him about Marnie's mother's case."

My head starts throbbing. "No, I never did get around to calling him. How do you know he's missing?"

"Well, initially one of his friends let us know that he'd missed his weekly ballgame watch they do together, but since it'd only been twenty-four hours at that point since the last time he'd been seen, no formal report was filed. But then the next Monday, Sowers never showed for his shift, so some uniforms went over to his house and found some suspicious things. That's when the investigation formally started."

"What suspicious things?"

"Er, well…" Gary looks up at Marnie's closed front door, then lowers his voice. "Just between you and me, pictures of girls. Lots of them. And not senior portraits, if you catch my drift. Plus numerous pairs of women's underwear, each of them in their own separate plastic bag. That's when they found the journals. From what they say, looks like he was a serial rapist and been doing it for years."

"You're kidding me."

"Wayne, I'm telling you all this out of professional courtesy, but right now they aren't revealing any of this to the public until the investigation is over."

"Yeah, I'll keep it under my hat, no problem."

Gary looks off in the distance to the corn fields. "Those look overdue. Surprised Marnie hasn't started harvesting them. She's usually on top of things like that."

"I'll be sure to mention it to her," I say.

## 22

# the gift

<u>Marnie</u>

I'm sitting in my truck at Grants Pass Airport. I'm five minutes early for the 3:30 appointment. His office is inside of a small hangar. I enter the hangar and knock on the outside of the open door and die with embarrassment when I recognize the man.

The man looks up, "It's YOU," and throws down his pen on top of his desk and shakes his head.

"I'm sorry, Mr. Gavin, I didn't mean to—"

"What do you want?"

"Ahh, my son wants to learn how to fly." I can't believe it's Ted Gavin, the same man from the diner three week ago, that I accused of raping me. I feel my face flushing.

"How old is he?" Gavin picks up a pen and takes an application form out of his desk; but the whole time he won't look at me.

"Sixteen, but I know lessons are expensive. I'm wondering if there's a way, we could pay for some and he could work here part-time for a portion of them? I spoke to Principal Palmer at the High

School and he said something like that might be possible. He said you went to the same high school."

"I did, why does your son want to fly?" he asks, finally lifting his head.

"He wants to go into aeronautics, get a college degree in something related flying." Gavin taps his pen on his desk.

"What kind of student is he?"

"He's very smart, but you wouldn't guess it from some of his grades."

"Sounds like how I used to be. Have your son, come in himself and talk to me. Hopefully, he's less of a screwball than his mother."

"Ahh, no guarantees on that," I say.

"What's your son's name?"

"Cole Tillman."

"Have him stop by tomorrow, at 4:00 and I'll speak with him," Gavin says. "I'm sure we can work something out."

"Thank you, Mr. Gavin, and again, I'm sorry—"

"It's Ted and apology accepted."

I can't wait to get home and tell Cole he has interview for a job that would allow him to take flying lessons.

"THANK YOU SO MUCH, MARNIE, FOR THE GIFT YOU LEFT FOR ME AND Bob," Mrs. Bradley says. My mind races. I hardly slept at all last night, I was so nervous about meeting with Mrs. Bradley and her friend. "It's so charming. I put it in my curio cabinet." She points with pride to it. I remember admiring the cabinet when I stayed in the house, displaying various pieces of ceramics and blown glass. She gestures to the other woman sitting with us. "This is my friend Janet Courtland. She owns Courtland Galleries in Portland."

"It's nice to meet you," the woman says. "Were you able to bring some of your other pieces with you?"

"Yes," I reply, taking my rocks out of the bag and laying them out on the table. "I only brought fifty, but I have hundreds more at home."

"How long have you been an artist?" Janet asks as she picks one up and admires it.

I blush. "Oh, well, 'artist.' I don't consider myself that. This is just something I do to keep myself from going crazy. I don't have an art degree or anything like that."

"You don't have to have professional training to be an artist. It's a calling." She begins looking the pieces over. "Do you draw all your inspiration from nature?"

"Yes, most of it, so far. It seems to make the most sense, since rocks come from nature. Years ago I once found an oval shaped rock on my farm, bleached almost completely white, and later that night I was sitting on the front porch when I heard an owl. I remembered the rock, which reminded me of a snow owl, so I painted that. That was the first one. Some rocks seem to just communicate to me somehow what they're meant to be."

"How interesting. How much do you price them for?"

"Oh, I've never sold them. I just give them away anonymously. I leave them around in random locations for others to find, like the one Mrs. Bradley found here, at her place."

"Oh, my dear," Janet says, smiling. "We could sell these at the gallery easily for $300.00 a piece."

"For a painted rock?"

"They're more than just paint on a rock. I can see your soul in each and every one of these. So can everyone else. That's what people are paying for. How many do you currently have completed?"

"I'm not sure. A couple hundred right now, I think?"

"Let's see." She looks up in the air, doing calculations in her head. "At three hundred per, minus our 25 percent commission, of course, that would be…$45,000 for you for the first show."

"The *first* show?"

The two women look at each other, then both gently giggle.

"Marnie," Janet says, turning again to me, "welcome to the first day of the rest of your life."

I leave the house with my head spinning. Forty-five thousand dollars per show? That could let me stop the pot growing altogether. This could finally be a way out, for all of us.

### Marnie

"I'M HAPPY YOU'RE GOING WITH ME TO THE FINAL MEETING WITH RICO and Diego at Jack & Jills tonight," and I hug Wayne. "I was going to invite Kate too, but I haven't been able to get ahold of her. I spoke to her last week and she told me about some new guy she was head over heels about."

"You know how she is," Wayne replies, rubbing my shoulders. "She could have run off to Key West for a weekend."

"It's possible, but I still think she would have called. Another weird thing…I haven't heard anything from Derek either."

"That is strange. I could check into it. Thank God the harvest went fine and the fungus you worried about from the streams never reached the main fields," Wayne says.

"Yeah. Rico's men will package the finished product next week, and then I'll be free of them for good. By the way, Janet Courtland called. She's already sold seven of my pieces. Can you believe it?"

"Yes, I can. I told you you're talented." Wayne kisses me as the sun shines through the glass window and warms us.

"I never thought anything like this was possible." I take a rock out and run my hands over it, letting it speak to me and tell me what it should be. I place it on the table and arrange my paints. I put all my colors on the palette because nature is made of all colors. Wayne pours me a cup of coffee, and sits beside me and Nova lays down under the table at our feet. For the first time since my mother's murder and my rape so many years ago, I feel safe. I reach over and take his hand. I'm finally with the man I love, the one I was meant to be with from the start—my first love, Wayne Farr. "Do you want to go in the bedroom and try our new water bed?"

Wayne tilts his head, and his eyes meet mine, "I thought you'd never ask."

### The End

# epilogue

<u>Marnie</u>

When Wayne and I enter Jack and Jill's, Rico and Diego stand and hold out their hands, but there's a much older man sitting at the table who doesn't do either. I've never met him before. He's got slicked-back white hair and a matching goatee, and he's slouched back casually in his chair like he's the king of the room. The man's wearing a white shirt covered with white embroidery, navy-blue pants and black loafers.

"We were hoping you would come, Wayne," Rico says. "This is my brother Diego, and my father, Ricardo Rojo." Wayne and I nod our heads and we all sit down. "The yield is good, considering this was your first grow, Marnie."

"And her last," Wayne adds.

Diego's eyes narrow. "It doesn't work that way. We've made a substantial investment in Marnie and her property. She doesn't stop until we're done with her."

"And if she doesn't continue?" Wayne asks, standing.

"All of you, stop talking about me like I'm not here." I stare at everyone at the table.

Rico smiles. "Direct as always. So I'll be direct too. We have your friend Kate. If you ever want to see her again, Marnie, you will cause no trouble."

I jump up from the table. "What did you do with her?" I should have anticipated Rico taking her. *Stupid, Marnie, stupid.*

"She's safe for now," Rico says. "I don't think Kate believes bad things could ever happen to her. You wouldn't want to destroy her world view, would you? Both of you should sit." Their father, silent the entire time, watches Rico with an expression of satisfaction on his face.

"You tricked her," I say as both of us take our seats.

"I seduced her, which requires two willing participants. I'm surprised she didn't tell you that we were dating. Perhaps she didn't want you to judge her. You're quite good at that."

"Shut your mouth."

"Now, now, don't grow defensive. I'm just 'giving you the skinny,' as the American gangsters say. Kate's been living with me for a few days now and is quite happy. She's a rather fun time, although an expensive one. I had to promise a weekly allowance to convince her to quit the diner."

"I want to speak to her."

"Do what you're told and you can," Rico says. "200 plants this next growing period. Believe me, this is still a very small amount, compared to what our other growers produce, but I know your concerns and appreciate them."

"How? They won't mature in time, it will get too cold. "

"You can use your barn and lights to grow them," Rico says with a curt nod.

"I've already told you. I don't want to draw attention to my farm by using electricity."

"We'll help you," Diego says. "We've purchased micro wind turbines to power the lights required," pressing his lips together.

"They'll be installed next week behind the barn. No one will even see them from the road," Rico says.

"You can't be serious?"

"We are," Rico says, staring me down.

"And you're going to hold Kate the entire time?" I ask, my voice shaking.

"Again, who is being held? Kate's having a splendid time in my company."

"Are you going to hurt her?"

"I promise you, be good and I won't have to." Rico stands, "By the way your friend Derek…you don't need to worry about him anymore either," he says with a playful grin.

"What do you mean?" Wayne asks, frowning.

"You didn't know about him? Rico asks. Wayne shakes his head. "How about you, Marnie?"

"He didn't follow my rules."

Rico chuckles, "He didn't follow mine either, Marnie. DEA, unfortunately, but luckily, we made him disappear long before he could report back to his people and do any damage. Marnie, Wayne, it's always a pleasure seeing you." Diego and Ricardo stand, too. The three of them walk out the door, leaving Wayne and I to just stare at each other.

"That went exactly like we knew it would," Wayne says, with as much sarcasm as he could muster.

"Not exactly. I didn't think it was even a possibility that they'd take Kate." I cover my eyes with my hands. My stomach feels hard and I feel like throwing up.

"I know you're worried, but you know she has a way of handling herself with men," Wayne says.

"Yes, she twists them around her little finger." We get up from the table and cross the bar to see Gary.

"Did you get all that, Gary?" Wayne asks.

"Clear as day," Gary says and takes out the earpiece.

Wayne removes the recorder that was in his jacket. "You're going to have to get a message to the DEA about Derek. I can't do it."

"No problem. Did any of them seem suspicious?" Gary asks.

"No, they didn't have a clue, that we were taping them." Wayne says.

"Good thing. I don't think these guys would hesitate to kill you, Marnie, Kate, Marnie's kids, and everyone you know if you caused them trouble. Are you sure this is the way you want to play it?"

"There's no other way to play it. We need hard evidence if we're going to put them away," Wayne says.

"Why don't we call in your buddies at the FBI?"

"No, it's too early, we need more. Hopefully my people are still doing their jobs, and together we'll bury them once we put all the pieces together," Wayne says.

"Your call," Gary says. "But be careful. You're playing for keeps now."

"But, Kate is caught in the middle of this. If something goes bad. What's going to happen to her? I ask.

### Rico

It's quiet in the car as Manuel drives them back to the hotel. Finally the man who thinks he's Rico's father speaks. "You outmaneuvered both of them, Rico. The ex-FBI agent isn't likely to do anything. He wants to protect the woman because he doesn't want her to suffer any legal ramifications, and the woman won't tell anyone because she's worried about your new whore, her friend. You played it well."

"She's more than that."

"If that is the case, get rid of her soon. Be more like your brother —fuck them a few times and find a new one. Eventually you'll find one from a reputable family to provide you with children, but that day is not here yet."

"What time is your flight?" my brother interrupts.

"Two p.m. I'll be away for a month. When I get back, this Kate woman should be gone. Are we clear on what that means, Rico?"

"Yes, Poppa." Rico nods in agreement, but doesn't look at him.

They pull up in front of the hotel, and the two brothers watch their father enter. "He did the same thing to me with Rita," Diego says, his eyes saddening. "Perhaps by the time he returns, you'll be tired of the woman and it will be easier to do what he commands."

"Was it easy for you?" Rico asks.

"No, but I did it. You can't say no to poppa, you know how he is."

"Even if that is so, how do you think Marnie is going to react to me killing her friend? Then we will have to kill her FBI boyfriend next, and at that point we will have a big mess on our hands." Rico thinks again about whether now is the right time to finally reveal that Ricardo is not his father. Rico leans back and lights a cigar, struck by the rare occurrence of not knowing what to do next.

*Will Wayne re-join the FBI?*
*Will Wayne tell the FBI about Marnie's misdeeds?*
*Will the law catch up with Rico & his family?*
*Will Marnie and Wayne continue their relationship or will it implode?*
*Will Marnie's pot growing enterprise continue to thrive?*
*Will Rico choose Kate or his family?*

*Read Book 2, Seeds of Justice in The Flower Queen Series:*
*coming Spring 2025 to learn the answers!*

# about the author

Kay Freeman spent the early part of her career as a professional artist. She's shown her work throughout the United States under her professional name, Kay A. Klotzbach. Kay was a full-time art professor in South Jersey for over twenty-three years and was granted a Princeton Mid-Career Fellowship for her teaching and her community based service learning projects.

Kay decided to pursue her passion for writing after her manuscript, *Truth Moon*, was selected by Romance Writers of America's RAMP program in 2021, which led to the publication of her debut novel, *Truth Moon*, by The Wild Rose Press. Kay has gone on to self-publish four other novels. She also writes a publication for romance authors, *What Do Romance Authors Think About,* a free newsletter on Substack.

Besides her passion for art, reading, and writing, she loves the blues, tequila, her husband Barry, and her standard poodle, Tango. This list is not intended to be in any particular order. Kay lives in Wilmington, DE.. You can learn more at KaylaaFreeman.com